too much flesh
and Jabez

Those who are by nature the victims must
bear a punishment in addition.
—JAKOB WASSERMANN, *The World's Illusion*

COLEMAN DOWELL

too much flesh and Jabez

A New Directions Book

Portions of this work first appeared in *Ambit* (London), to whose editors and publisher grateful acknowledgment is made.

Manufactured in the United States of America
First published as New Directions Paperbook 447 in 1977
Published simultaneously in Canada by Clelland & Stewart, Ltd.

Library of Congress Cataloging in Publication Data

Dowell, Coleman.
  Too much flesh and Jabez.
  (A New Directions Book)
  I. Title.
PZ4.D7396TO   [PS3554.0932]   813'.5'4   77–1631
ISBN 0–8112–0658–0 pbk.

New Directions Books are published for James Laughlin
by New Directions Publishing Corporation,
333 Sixth Avenue, New York 10014

For Bert and Tam and Edmund

Even after the tale had been rewritten to her satisfaction she could not quite leave it alone. She tried locking it away and misplacing the key, a game that afforded some amusement for it paralleled the fact that in her rereadings of her creation she could find less and less of herself, so that she was like the lost key. Thinking to have found herself in one character she would, without warning, "become" another: now Jim, now Jabez, now Ludie, and so on, but she had an increasing sense of insecurity in her own persona, which like an amoeba had divided into two and then gone on subdividing. She did not know if blame could be placed on her age or on the confusions resulting from having written, at such an age, the perverse story. She thought that it might be because the brutality of the direct gaze was not endurable in daily existence, and so she turned to vagaries and obliqueness.

So the tale continues. I am setting this down, I tell myself, to "frame" the story—an old device—but the search is dead earnest. I can imagine getting lost altogether.

The obliqueness was like, as she termed it, a trinocular, allowing for the existence and employment of the third eye, through which she could look at peripheries and only occasionally, when the third lens opened, at the result of some self-discoveries. One eyepiece showed her her talent for narrative; another revealed a prurience which was no real surprise at such a late date; the third eyepiece forced her to see that she would have been—was, indeed, being—a monstrous juror: out of tidbits of town gossip and some exchanged glances and silences between what she thought of as "the defendants in the case," she had created a world as dark as many encoun-

I

tered in her secret reading, those books as difficult of access, in her isolationist world, as were the darker reaches of herself.

Some details of the writing pleased her. One of these was the way she had woven herself, at last and apparently inextricably, into the fabric of Jim's life. Each scene in which she appeared was a signature like Whistler's butterfly. That these were distorted, were a concealment, she saw as a clever stratagem (as though Jim might read the tale!). A more bitter satisfaction was in the surfacing into words of her loathing of the type of woman she had had to deal with all of her life. (In the "authorial" voice she appeared as a stranger amid aliens when in fact she was of them by birth and upbringing.)

She was never able to think realistically about her retirement. When it came, when it was forced upon her at the age of seventy, she felt that the stuff of life had been taken from her: felt, the perfect word, for the information had been given and received viscerally. She had not believed that she could survive the first long winter of inactivity. It was then that she had begun setting down her memories, and again it seemed that the frequently distasteful pursuit was like examining visceral specimens collected over the years and preserved away from the corrupting light. The analogy seemed a perfect one for old age, for its demoralized degradation and the way it refuted one's mental life by turning not upward to the realm of philosophy but downward into facts, immutable, of nature.

In her scribblings there re-emerged one figure beside which all but her parents paled to outlines: Jim Cummins, on whom she had pinned long-dormant hopes for four years, to whom she had devoted openly and sometimes controversially the major share of her attention, whom she had, at her initial insistence, tutored privately. She recalled, the recalling like the virgin experience, the intensity of her pleasure the first time he asked for her services. To this end she gave her week ends as required, and for a time their mutual ambitions for him took all of her week ends, with Jim staying in a room on her street. It went without saying that there was talk of an ugliness endemic to isolationist towns. Their week ends were confined to summer, Saturday nights, and Sundays, so there was no conflict with Jim's active athletic life in the school year and his farmer duties in the planting and reaping seasons. Thus the spitefulness of the faculty gossip was in all ways groundless, and yet it was the conflicting gossip that brought to an end *the only satisfactory association she had ever had with a pupil.* But that astounding fact did not emerge until she put it beneath the microscope of her retirement and watched it wriggle for month upon snowbound month.

Her pain at Jim's desertion had been filed away in a drawer labeled "Discipline," and she had gone on about her business, impassive under the curious collective eye of the faculty and student body.

Reseeing her last meeting with Jim, nearly ten years before her retirement, when he reeled up to her on the street, as drunk as anyone she had ever seen, she sought to find the material for self-derision in her belief that she could have molded out of the farmboy someone to fit her specifications. Her ambition for him had been political. In him she would implant the seeds from which would grow a legislator to lead all the others to bring about changes in a state as badly run, considering the needs of its people, as a medieval fiefdom.

She had instructed Jim in the plight of the miners, taught him, veiling the lesson in the tatters and rents of recent history, that the Red Camps springing up everywhere were the logical results of what was going on in the state and Federal capitals. She personally introduced him to the specter of starvation in the midst of plenty, skeletons growing from a fat land, which she compared to Cadmus' army reverting to dragon's teeth in the stupid land of Thebes.

She knew that she had not mistaken the capacity of his brain, which she saw as abnormally large, an organ too large for his own good, probably, considering the life he chose despite her and the company he kept: the wearisomely stupid "good old boys" of all Southern small towns. Who could accommodate the outsize brain? and she visualized his suffering as he sought vainly to use it, and was bemused to find so unambiguously in herself the talent for sexual metaphor. Or did the nuances of "abnormally large organ" lie in some dimly heard gossip about him in the corridors—not heard, but glimpsed, that implication, rising, enclosed in a comic-strip balloon, from a cluster of headbent girls?

But she had failed with him, and in her speculations she wondered if the failure had been in mistaking the quality of his mind which caused her to lay stresses externally, so to speak, where the dura mater was thickest, in her haste forgetting the arachnoid and the pia mater, which would have been like a schoolmarm whipping a boy with a pillow in his trousers. "How could I have got it through his thick head!" was a cliché that haunted her, and she became obsessed by the thought that method alone had stood between her and the goals she had set for them both. Yet how could she have taught him indifference to public opinion while at the same time instilling in him awareness of the needs, and thus the voice, of the people?

Hardly had the winter ended—beginning, just, to merge into a cold spring—when her obsession drove her to visit the Cummins Place, as she learned it was called, in a section not remote in distance but, she saw once she was there, curiously untouched by time, or by the times that had so violently affected the town in which she lived and where she had taught him for his four years in the high school.

The handsome house was in a state of repair that bespoke other times when paint and shingles had been in plenty for those who could afford them. The fences she could see bore no winter ravages and the lawn, showing evidence of a recent rolling, was vaporous with the green of new grass.

Standing beside her car, taking the measure of the land, she saw the artful lie of the house in relation to sun, prevailing wind, water, and protective hills, and was stirred by evidence of intelligence. The country that had spawned Jim and herself was a haphazard one in which houses regularly destroyed by flood were rebuilt on the same spot, or, conversely, were placed so far from water that the young were pack animals

4

by the age of five. She noticed the deep-cut wagon road which would carry runoff from the fields. Then, painful as a wrench to a muscle, a distortion came into her vision which made her envisage the road swollen in flood; astonished, she watched from afar as her imagination placed upon its tide a boat like a hearse drawn by swimming black horses, plumed heads tossing.

As though seeking the source of such outrageousness, she looked toward the house, and her eyes were drawn to the pulled-aside window curtain; smiling at not having thought that she might be observed observing, or, as it must have looked (and was!) spying, she advanced to the house with the apologetic step of old age.

Watching the slow opening of the door as she stepped onto the veranda, she was excited to have no thought of what might lie behind it. Even as she explained to herself the unlikely romance of the thought through reminders of her first winter alone, the little mystery was dispelled at once by the small direct woman holding out her hand, identifying herself as Effie Cummins, Jim's wife. The teacher handed over her own identity as though presenting a gift to the wrong person, for Effie was woefully plain, the last type Jim could have been expected to settle for: a dry little bird with sparse feathers.

But her welcome was eager if voluble. "Wind shifted to the east in the night, I reckon you noticed! Wonder to me you didn't freeze, that wind setting at your back. Come in, come in, there's a fire in the parlor." Coffee was offered and taken along with a piece of light, still warm, cake, the ritual performed without a pause in the chatter, Effie's voice rising and falling as she came and went, rising, when she was two rooms away, to a stridency that made the teacher smile at this evidence of country loneliness.

"I'm sometimes thankful for an east wind, though they do say it's a time when more old people die." (I nodded: a naturally tactless woman, Jim's wife, or clever at compliments.) "My reason's that it gives me an excuse to keep a fire in here in the daytime. Jim's mother, now, she kept fires going no matter where the wind lay. But seems to me like they had more chances to be ladies back then, what with all the help

5

—ours gone off now in the War, of course. I reckon Mister Hitler has equalized the Southland, black just as good as white when it comes to cannon fodder." As though apologizing for thought, Effie added, " 'Least, that's what Jim says." (I thought, without charity, that such a deduction would not have occurred to a woman like her.)

The teacher learned that Effie had recognized her, for Jim had "once or twice" pointed her out on the street. "Myself, I went to Locust Grove School, but they tore it down years back. It's all county high schools nowadays. Jim was lucky to go to a town school, I reckon, but me, I never cared much for learning, though I'm ashamed to tell it." But she spoke rather smugly.

"What did you care about?"

"Like just about every other girl, I wanted to make a good marriage."

"And you have." The teacher spoke as though there could be no argument. When immediate corroboration was not forthcoming she looked up from her plate, where she had been gathering crumbs, in surprise. She saw that Effie was no liar, for under her gaze Effie did not rush in with belated agreement. It seemed that the evidence for a good marriage was spread out between the two women like wedding gifts which they labeled in silence: Jim's good looks, his property and family name, his intelligence (in the order of their importance to Effie, I thought); perhaps he was faithful, too, for she had heard no talk to the contrary. Faintly recalling some gossip about another family member, she said, "Jim has a sister, I think?"

"Clara married a Northerner and lives up there."

It did not seem to be what she sought, but Effie did not continue. The teacher wondered if it was out of ignorance of the gossip. A silence fell between them. To fill it the teacher spoke of her retirement. She told Effie that after a sedentary winter she had begun a series of little trips, when she could get the gasoline, to look up old pupils. The lie did not bother her. Truthfully, she told Effie that she had learned through inquiry of Jim's deferment and so had known that the trip would not be wasted. She said this as one prudent woman to another, setting the unspoken "patriotic" between them like a cozy bond, for she imagined that Effie was sentimental in that direction. It was an aimless effort; there could be no bond between an Effie and herself. But some inner communication apparently was possble, for as soon as the teacher rejected the idea of a bond, Effie got up abruptly and led her to the screened-in back porch and gave curt instructions on how to find Jim.

And then it was as though Effie was willing to trust a stranger with her vulnerability rather than face it alone.

Her last words were intriguing for their tone and for something confused in the motions of the hands, as though pushing at an invisible thing, which framed them. "He might not be by himself."

Was it embarrassment? The teacher decided that that was closest. And it carried over into the first moments of her meeting with Jim, who was by himself.

She let excitement take her as she walked where she had been instructed to walk, into the deep country of fallow fields outlined by lanes which in turn were defined by dense growth of natural fences composed of scrub, ancient and twisted. She thought the scrub was like a manifestation of man's reasons for seeking dominance over wild-running nature. The quixotic shift of her sympathy to nature's side became part of the excitement, part of the continuance of the romance that began with the funereal image. Walking here was like treading a complex map in bas-relief, a dry run for a long sojourn in a place so recently charted that this was the only copy. To ally oneself with all the elements of nature at this time was expedient!

I recall that I felt not young but ageless, and freed somehow, and I agreed with myself—beginning even then to divide, I see—that I would be the one to go native if given the chance.

Turning, or so it seemed, within herself, it was as though she found Jim at the center of a maze. She saw him looming far down a lane, and her heart was moved. Here was the object, like an artifact sought in a jungle, that had been her impetus, or so it seemed, for survival of the terrible winter.

I remember saying, "Don't expect too much," meaning of him. After that I really did become "in the third person." Self victim? I still don't know.

She called his name and then hers.

The changes in him were personified by his unwillingness to look at her direct. In her winter memories the compelling gaze of his eyes, as though willing one to be more and more explicit until nothing was left unsaid, had assumed, she saw, legendary proportions: the gaze of a great mesmerist which could draw your knowledge from you—and she saw that she had metamorphosed him into the teacher, herself into the pupil. Her journey then was in quest of what he could tell her about herself.

"I've missed you foolishly," she told him. "I've had reveries in which you saved the world, and I wanted to have a look at the Messiah."

She thought: the face of such a man doesn't crumple under strain. What does it do, what is it doing?

"What about myself?" he asked.

"What?"

"Did I save myself, in your reveries? Or just the world?"

Carefully she told him, "Well, you are the world, Jim, and I am. Our first thoughts are for ourselves, even if we don't want to admit it. Altruism is just the other face of ego."

And she drew him out, and they spoke, and she left, pleading, if he could have heard, for an invitation to return, which was not forthcoming. He walked with her a way, showing her a short cut. As they parted she thought that she had got her invitation, for in response to her question about the load of work without field hands, he mentioned his loneliness, or the isolation, or said it was not the extra work he minded so much. Afterward she could not recall his words.

She was confused by the turns her mind kept taking in the next week, at the meanings she persistently tried to read into the exchanges with Effie and Jim, and what the silences came to represent to her. It was nearer an unrequited longing for gossip than philosophical speculation. In a kind of fury at the three of them, she set off for her second visit to the Cummins Place.

The changes the week had wrought were immediately apparent in Effie's attitude, which could only be termed evasive. She was not sure where Jim was, or that he was on the place at all. He had said something about a trip to Salvation, but she had been too busy to pay attention. She did not think the visitor would want to strike out and try to cover the place looking for Jim, on such a muddy day, not sure of finding him at all. But the spring thaw, thank the Lord, had finally set in, and a body could start thinking about her garden.

In a pause in the flow the teacher asked maliciously, "Is Jim alone today?" Effie's face brought to mind clear and brightly lighted an episode of sixty years back when a girl, refused permission to leave the classroom, sat pissing in her chair. That humiliation had found its perfect twin today. In consternation the teacher put out her hand to Effie as she could not have to the stricken girl, who had been herself.

Slogging through the mud in her heavy overshoes she could find nothing to like in herself, past, present, or, she suspected, future, and so was freed of another burden. She imagined herself hunched over her desk writing anonymous letters of a scurrility unmatched in the county where the practice was famous. She had received a number, all because of Jim, toward whom she headed with revenge on her mind. No, upon her spirit, which was wilted like a plant in a long drought. What the plant wanted was not water but to be cut down, for revival would be long and probably painful, and new growth, what there was of it, would be stunted and useless.

Her merciless eyes found Jim's silhouette and traced down it, looking for the fat that must have been concealed by his coat a week ago, the mysterious early flab of hardworking farmers. It was as though that part her eyes sought gathered itself together and detached, trying to slink away, for as she watched, Jim became two distinct creatures, and then she saw that the result of his apparent dehiscence was a long-haired child. As she approached, the child wandered off; it satisfied her to think that its departure was connected with her. She chose later on to believe that she could see the directive on Jim's lips, each time erasing the fact that she could not have seen either of their faces because they stood against the brightness of the east.

She did not care that there was no welcome, and she offered no explanation for her second visit, thinking "tit for tat." When Jim moved, she moved with him, down the gullylike lane where spring fires, bases protected from the wind, threw up straight spouts of smoke which, meeting wind above the tops of scrub trees, split and streamed downward onto the tight buds like water from fountains.

Chatting, not caring a hoot what she said or how it was received, she observed how Jim kept looking in the direction of the child, who plowed steadily away, muddying its shoes with obvious pleasure by walking through puddles. Her heart caught at Jim's expression when the child, turning in profile to emphasize the maneuver, she told herself, bent over, hands clasped on its stomach. She concentrated on the child, determined to fathom some of its mystery. It stood like a statue, its hair swinging forward to cloak its face, the straining cloth of its clothes tracing lines of such tenderness that the teacher felt the powerful attraction of androgyny, like a self-memory. Was the attraction based on more than a hint of self-sufficiency, of not needing another person to complete it? Not everyone paired off like animals approaching the Ark, and the reason, in some cases, was a rare intelligence, which she thought she could read in the lineaments of the childish body. Angels were androgynous, though they bore masculine names. She made a mental note: Think out.

When she looked again at Jim she saw that he was stooping a little and held out his hands as though for a baby to step into them.

She was inwardly informed that she had seen enough, that to stay around would be to expose herself to obscenity. She was astonished by such an extreme thought. For a moment she was able to view similar excesses of the past week including the hearse-boat and the anger that had propelled her to make today's journey, but the new sensibility would brook no prolonged interference. Feeling inhabited, with bare civility she bade Jim adieu. When she had gone a few feet he called after her, "Miss Ethel—" It was a concerned voice from the past. Not caring to look at him again, she inclined her head, giving him permission to proceed. "Are you all right?" But his question had been in the way he spoke her name, was unnecessary to an extent that made her reply sound contemptuous: "Of course I am."

Returning, she felt her years in every bone. She constructed scenes: Jim and the child; herself, Jim, and the child; herself and the child—and the latter was like being alone with herself.

In the scene that she kept, Jim asked the child, "When you bent over back there, what did you think you'd found?" The child answered, its voice maintaining the necessary androgyny, "A violet. Knew it couldn't be. Just a piece of colored glass." On Jim's face she placed the desire to uproot all the violets in the world and give them to the hermaphrodite, if they could feed the thin regret in the words.

Effie was airing quilts on a clothesline, and Miss Ethel found extremely unattractive the way the woman tried to hide from her among the patchwork, like a cricket in a field. Aiming her words at the woman's feet she called out "Good day again," putting into the words what malice she could. Her wish of less than an hour ago to apologize to Effie was gone. The secretiveness of the encounters rankled the way notes passed under her nose between students had once inflamed her temper, famous, for all the liberality of her classes in other respects.

"I found him," she addressed the feet, which then moved. Effie's face, emerging from the corridor of quilts, was set, as though it had stiffened to withstand an expected slap.

"S'what you came for." She laughed, not really unpleasantly, Miss Ethel thought, admiring the skill of that laugh, and asked, in what seemed to be a frontal attack, "I imagine Bessie was with him?"

"No," Miss Ethel said. "He was alone," and she waited. If she knew her quarry, it would make a revealing move. Effie, tougher than she would have thought, showed only slight surprise, but her words were more satisfactory.

"Still sick, then. Helentaylor said this morning—" Whether the teacher's too obvious interest caused the halt, she could not have said.

"Bessie is Helen Taylor's child?"

"Kin," Effie said uncomfortably with a look that had the appearance of shame. "Some say 'Bessie,' mean younguns, if a body can believe one word—" She took Miss Ethel's breath by saying without transition, "Go on back to town, Miss Ethel. Quit your snooping around here!" She ran to the house, her rubber boots and the mud sucking together.

In the car, the expenditure of energy caught the teacher up in trembling, and she was afraid for herself because of the sharpness of her wish for a feast of revenge, denied her at the Cummins Place, and now the larder was locked because of ineptitude which let her show them her hunger. She thought that her hunger was based entirely upon a life of every kind of denial except that of thought. "And of that," she said, "too goddamned much."

Yet soon enough she came to believe that there had been too little. Amid the sounds of spring cleaning all around her she sat in her winter squalor and let the setting of what she would examine in fine invented detail take her: the loneliness of the farm and the sense of some darkness still remote and anomalous, toward which one would have to advance to examine it, for it was stationary like a horizon, incapable of movement of its own, for which she could be thankful. She asked herself, "Why thankful?" and replied, "The child." For it was in the direction of children that duplicity and revenge lay.

She relived the duality of her own youth, her toughening (into androgyny, she thought) at the hands and minds of five wild brothers and a pack of equally wild male cousins, the way she had had to conceal the calluses from her suspicious mother. Her early ease of concealment cast an acid light upon her life. The hellion she saw moving about in the nineteenth century was recognizably herself; hardly any chipping was required, after the first tries, at the gloss of her formal education that was like hardened icing on a cake, for huge chunks came away intact, and beneath, unharmed by a burial of over fifty years, cavorted the blunt-languaged hoyden of her youth.

Then, her primary question had been addressed to masculine experience: "What is it like?" Answers were always provided, sarcastically, teasingly, soberly (was he a cousin or a brother?), sometimes with another heat that could have engulfed her. Always, the language was plain and rough. Nothing she had since read, in Caldwell and that ilk or in books that came to her in plain wrappers, had surpassed its Chaucerian clarity. She longed for those untrammeled days, those companions, for her youth. To start over! The plaint of humanity.

Sitting by late lamplight she practiced. Pursing her mouth, she would say, "Sexual intercourse" and then "fuck," and note how the latter word loosened her mouth, freed it. She enjoyed the muscular laxness like that following laughter. "Self-abuse," "jack off."

One day in the drugstore as she drank a lemon Coke she forgot her whereabouts and performed one of her liberating exercises in public.

After that she was aware of people watching her, heard how they spoke about her in her hearing as though she were either deaf or retarded. She found that this was a freedom too, for in her sleuthing about Jim and others she could be as direct as she chose. "In school," she inquired of an old pupil, "was Jim what you could call a cocksman?" She did not mind that the reply was enveloped by the usual buzz that made a group or individual sound like swarming flies.

On lucid days it was not easy to accept the lack of respect that let them refer to her as "nutty as a fruitcake." She was tempted to explain that whatever obsessed her was, she believed, temporary like a case of the 'flu; but as summer lengthened her seizures correspondingly grew, and by late July she was hardly venturing forth at all. Her customary stance was to sit hunched over her lined tablets as though at any moment she might be impelled to set upon them some mark that would turn out to be definitive.

One night she awoke from a dream as fresh as experience. She was embarked upon a trip back to the Cummins Place, she arrived, she saw the wild grasses taking over the fields, found dilapidation wherever she looked. In the dream Effie was entirely uncommunicative. She did not ask Jim's old teacher into the house but stood blocking the doorway. The yearning to get inside the house, to wander through its rooms, was like all the desires of the teacher's life rolled into a rug with herself inside. Craning past Effie, their two cheeks touching, Miss Ethel saw dust where there had been shine, saw, though it was high summer, an uncleaned grate, the chimney's fauces clogged with soot that hung untidily. Jim would not have let that happen. She could feel his absence. Where was he? Traveling with the child. An inner journey?

She asked, "Is the child still sick? Is it, perhaps, expected to die?"

"I hope so," poor Effie said, beginning to close the door on the stench. But the teacher craned further, over Effie's shoulder. She saw in the clutter evidence of a woman totally alone like herself, one who, having only herself to please, finds it the same as having no one, nothing, pleasure least of all. Recalling her spurious try at placing a bond between herself and Effie on her first visit she saw that now they had not one bond but two.

At dawn she began to clean her house. For days she cleaned and waxed and painted, humming toward the end of the siege. Observing the results, she told herself, "Now."

She prepared to enter herself, maybe to find, behind the new paint and wax, what Jim seemed to have pointed out to her: the stalactites and stalagmites of a selfishness that might turn out to be extraordinary. For she had never once entered another person, and no other person had ever entered her.

14

TOO MUCH FLESH AND JABEZ

I

The dinner bell rang across the dusty tobacco field, catching Jim between the shoulder blades like a rusty knife. He straightened up, one big paw full of suckers, and arched his spine, feeling the drought-parched air nudge into the curve to lap like a thirsty animal at the sweat of his back. From the reservoir of his thick hair under the felt hat which he wore summer and winter, water ventured to be caught just beneath the sweatband and sucked down to its salt. The rim of skin at the top of his forehead was tightened and stung by the salt until it felt as if he wore a crown of mosquitoes. He snatched the hat off, slapping it against the prickling skin, releasing a shower of sweat that spattered some leaves of tobacco with blightlike spots. Almost instantly, in the white heat, his hair was dry down to the scalp—thick, well-rooted hair that as a rule was shiny with natural oil which persisted through its twice-daily dunking, in the summertime, under the irony water of the pump.

The pump was now almost as dry as Jim's exposed head. He had to pass it by on his way to the house at dinnertime and at night, and scratch the salt from his head the way he had seen monkeys do, during his town days, feeling monkey-like himself, imprisoned behind bars of sun that seemed with each day to grow stronger.

That morning at the branch, dipping water into the barrels on the sledge, hearing with an ear that fought belief the scrape of the bucket against rocks, and him dipping from the deepest pool of the branch, he had looked at the rays of early sun falling through the trees, and it seemed to him as if they grew upward from the ground and were solid enough to be cut with a hatchet and used for firewood, or split into siding for a barn where the tobacco could be fired.

The drying tobacco scraped against Jim's crusted overalls as he walked to the wagon road, and he thought, "Firing itself in the field. Won't need a barn." Even if the drought miraculously ended in response to the prayer meetings being held, according to report, daily for that purpose, he did not see how he could chop the tobacco and hang it by himself, any more than he had been able to harvest his other money crop, the wheat, alone. The evidence of his failure, brittle and burnt, stretched around him so that he had to censor what he perceived or go in mourning through the days. If worse came to the very worst, he would have to concentrate on the fodder to see the animals through the winter, the way his wife was forced to neglect her flowers and pour all her energy along with the available water into the kitchen garden, to keep the two of them from starving.

He had to grin a little at the exaggeration—Effie's—of the food shortage, seeing in his mind the laden shelves in cellars and storerooms, the fruit jars in upstairs closets, the jam-packed smokehouses. Still, corncribs, barnlofts, and silos were low for this time of year, and there was no way to exaggerate the lack of help. With the War on there was no help to be had; none at all. Even the Negroes had been called up and came back on furloughs, strutting around in uniforms, some of them with stripes on their sleeves, while Jim, six-foot-four and two hundred twenty pounds of muscle, was left to fight the sun and the disappearing water by himself.

He stopped in the middle of the wagon road, heeding the eery silence the way he had not done for a long time, recalling that the dinner bell had been the first sound he had heard all morning, since he finished with the sledge and put it away. Not a sound came from the barns or pastures. His ears could not pick up a chicken scratch. He tried to think back to when he had last heard a bird sing or a crow caw.

It seemed to him that the sun and the War were alike, draining the countryside of life. If they went on long enough, without relief, they would drain the world. Maybe they already had, and only he and Effie did not know it.

He had spoken to no one except Effie for a week. He wondered if he and his wife were the only ones left, outlasting even the watchful crows.

He had a half-serious dread of going on up the road and around the stripping barn because that would bring him face to face with the henhouse, and he knew that for some reason he was vulnerable enough right then to keel over, and maybe die, if he saw one chicken dead on its back with its feet sticking up. There would be no time to look around for others that were not dead, or to listen for mothers clucking or grass widows singing. Over he would go, two hundred pounds plus of dead weight, and Effie, if she had not passed on first, would find him and give up the ghost, squawking and falling across him in the chicken do.

Or go back inside and run off with the soldier who had helped her plan Jim's death by catching all the birds and shutting them in the house, and bribing the neighbors to stay away (all but Helen Taylor, who would outlast death itself), and plucking the chicken, which they would eat with dumplings before they took off over the hill.

Jim slapped his hat back on, figuring himself to be just this side of a sunstroke and a damn fool for leaving his hat off for nearly five minutes, which was enough to give a man fever visions. The thought of a soldier wanting Effie, lurking around and acting in secret until he got her, was enough to bring a snort of laughter through his nose and with it some of the gummy phlegm that kept tobacco workers hawking and spitting like a ward of t.b. patients.

Still, probably because he had not put on the hat soon enough, when he started to turn by the stripping barn he felt the urge to look behind him, feeling peculiarly as if the emptiness were suddenly filled. Staring through the dust-brightened air, he told himself that it was like he had expected to see a row of heads lifting up from their work, hearing the bell tardily, and from a long time ago he did seem for a moment to be able to hear feet stamping dust from their shoes and a hawking as lungs were cleared against the prospect of grub. Instead of being scary, the trick his ears played was so comforting that he tried, by narrowing his eyes and pushing his imagination to the limit, to see the woolly heads freed of their straw hats, and the dark glistening skins, and his ears strained further to catch the rising murmur of voices as the common thought of food and rest restored the field hands to each other, and to him.

Then clearly, without distortion of any kind, he saw that he and someone were looking at each other across the distance. The person, a teen-age boy, it looked like, was standing leaning on the gate at the other end of the wagon road, but when its hand flew up in greeting Jim saw that the arm in the short-sleeved shirt was boneless as a girl's and that the hand fluttered like a caught bird. Something in Jim's breast matched the movement—a cluster of nerves, a pattern of muscles long unused—before he took hold and threw his hand up roughly and rounded the barn, wondering who the devil the trespasser was and how long she had been there watching him.

Tromping through the yard, ducking under the clothesline, scowling at the pump, he made himself think it was funny how fast he had gone from being one of the last lonesomest people left on earth to resenting a trespasser, and he was laughing when he slammed the door onto the back porch and went to the washbasin to clean up for dinner.

"Awh," Effie said behind him, sounding surprised the way she always did that it was him and not some horse that answered the dinner bell. He wished to his name, splashing furiously, that she would surprise him once in a while, with some other word or sound, instead of him always surprising her by coming home when she rang the bell. "Awh." She sounded like a chicken.

He thought about the chicken that was going to be the death of him, and Effie and her soldier, and began to splutter, snuffling water up his nose. Eyes squinched against the burning of tobacco-gummed water, his nose letting loose hot fluid to clean itself, which he sucked back up because he was laughing so hard, Jim groped for the roller towel and grabbed Effie instead by deliberate miscalculation.

"What on earth—" she said, not really curious, which told him that she had something on her mind, something she was waiting to spring on him when he had his mouth full at the table, hoping to finish him off by making him choke to death.

Effie was so little that Jim had to go on his knees to dry his face on her apron. A memory stirred in both of them; he could feel it in her withdrawal, and took his hands away before they could touch her below the waist. Still: "Je-im," she said, and he knew what was coming. "My Lord, what if somebody was looking!"

"There's nobody left but us," he mumbled in her apron, his beard and the starch rasping together until his beard won.

"What!" Effie said, her voice rising to a squeak, as if she believed him, and then, as he got to his feet, "Just look at that—" spreading the limp soiled apron over her two palms like a saleslady. She held the pose until she saw that it would lead nowhere, then followed Jim into the kitchen, taking covered dishes from the top of the stove as she passed, hurrying through the heat into the comparatively cool dining room where the shades were kept pulled against the glare. She made several trips back and forth for more food and cold milk, humming over her secret like a hen over a setting of eggs. Jim was too hungry to wait for her to sit down, but he loaded his mouth cautiously against the time when she let fly with her news.

Effie put a little of everything on her plate, nibbled, then said, casually, "Mama wrote—" and waited. Jim wanted to say, "Didn't know she could," but held his peace. The game was an old one: Effie offered bait, Jim refused it, Effie plunged in after him, floundering and gasping, holding out the whole can of worms, forgetting the hooks. Sometimes the tactic worked and she really hooked him, which was all she wanted from him, but from the way she held back on her opening he knew that today's news touched her where she lived, in her family pride, and he said, at the same time as Effie, "Junie—" and grinned maliciously at his wife's expression as she finished, "—'s getting married . . . how on *earth*—"

He shrugged, watching Effie's eyes die down, wondering who the sister had found who'd have her. Then, thinking about Junie's rounded little rear instead of her scrawny neck and buck teeth, he felt desire, and pity for his wife which let him ask, "Who'd she settle for?"

Effie was pleased because he implied that Junie had a choice, and her eyes lit up again as she rattled on, tamping down the part about her older sister's intended being old enough to have sired her, and hoeing up a hill when she got to the part about property. He made impressed sounds and Effie sailed off in triumph to get the letter.

Jim was sorry he had not had the gumption to take the victory when it was his, for now he would have to swallow the old woman's written words along with his dinner, and even second hand his mother-in-law's double talk gave him indigestion. Because whatever she wrote, however she built up the story of Junie's getting engaged, how ever many times the word love cropped up, Jim would see her engineering hand underneath, pulling strings and settling lives the way she had his, in cahoots with his own mother, dead last year, eight years too late.

He waited for the twinge that usually accompanied the ugly thought about his mother, but it did not come. If he had had the same control back then, when he was eighteen, the year he married Effie . . . but he had not. The two old women had been too much for him, especially, he thought, giving his dead mother what little loyalty he could summon—especially Effie's mother, for to her *property* was the answer to all questions. Certainly it was the motive for her pursuing and catching him for Effie.

He wondered if Effie ever looked back to their brief courtship and puzzled about it, as some other people had, because he did not need to be labeled vain to recognize that he had been considered a good catch, not all of it based on his property. He had played basketball in school and was called good-looking. Effie never had been. She was the kind of woman, bony and tight-skinned, who would reach her peak past fifty, when all the girls with bosoms and behinds had gone to fat. Even her thin hair would look more becoming to her age than the fluffy, girlish hair of the other women topping old faces. His mother had pointed that out to him, giving him (he had thought then and knew now) the choice between a skinny fifty-year-old wife and the farm, and a pretty, soft, eighteen-year-old bride and exile. And no property rights. Then who was he, condemning Effie's mother—an old question—when he had given up Ludie and married Effie to keep what he had?

For all his conviction in times of solitude, he would never know if the choice had really been given, or what would have happened if he had taken Effie out once and not gone back. He would never know if marrying him could have saved Ludie. All he knew was that he had been pressured, and believed himself to have been threatened, by his mother into courting Effie, had been twisted by Effie's mother in ways that only passing years had exposed, and that Ludie, whom he had gone on thinking of as "my girl" while he was dating Effie—that his girl Ludie had gone out of her mind and was locked away. The only souvenir he had of her was the scar where she bit him, white and puckered and thin-looking as a piece of tissue paper pasted to his thick shoulder.

He would have liked to stop there, and wanted Effie to come back and read him her mother's slanted words to cancel his thoughts with mockery, but his mind skittered on like a flivver on a washboard road.

Ludie had scarred him for life the night he tried to take her cherry, drunk and thinking that if he had it he could go on and marry Effie and please his mother, whose wishes he had been brought up to think were natural laws. Knowing that Ludie wanted him too, because she had said so time and again, and believing what he had been told from boyhood—that a man's cherry was as precious as a woman's—he had used his urgency to try to draw hers, and had told her he was going to marry Effie. He could feel the heat of her crotch on his hand, the one he had rammed home between her legs before she stopped him with her teeth white and sharp, her sweet spit burning him like venom.

It was the last time he saw her. A few weeks later she was carried away and locked up for life, first at home where she was not wanted, and then in the asylum. He asked her, "Did they want you there?"

"Well, sure, to help out and all." He had not heard Effie come back and sit down, did not know his eyes were closed until he opened them on her face turning apprehensive as he looked. "Jim, are you sick?"

He shook his head, coughed, and swallowed. "Why?"

"Sweat pouring off you in rivers."

"Summertime."

"Uh huh. I think you were going to sleep, 'swhat I think." She rustled the letter, cleared her throat, shot Jim another look, and smacked the letter down on the table with the flat of her hand.

"Aw, listen, go on and finish your dinner and go take a nap. You don't want to hear this letter now."

"Sure I do. Any old wedding of Junie's—"

"Go *on*, I said." Effie sounded quarrelsome, which showed her concern. Jim pushed back from the table, anticipating her next words.

"No pie," he said, then "Thanks," surprising them both. He got up and made it to the parlor door.

"Je-im." He stopped. "You sure you all right." He nodded.

"Sleepy's all. If I can make it to the yard 'fore I—" He forced a yawn, found to his relief that it went on and on. Effie came up behind him and slid under his arm.

"Let me help you, for Lord's sake. You hit the floor in your condition, go right through to the cellar."

They both pretended that she was supporting him to the door and out to the quilt spread under the oaks. He lowered himself onto his back, legs spread wide, hands cupping his head.

"Night."

"You." Her feet moved away, stopped. "I meant to ask—you see anybody this morning, passing through?"

"Through where."

"Wagon road, I reckon. Said I'd keep a lookout but forgot."

"Who for."

"Helentaylor's kin. Going to stay awhile. I was so full of Junie's wedding—" Jim's heart lifted up and knocked at his chest.

"Who—" His heart hammered three times against the word. He waited for Effie to ask what was the matter. She yawned; it seemed to go on through deliberation.

"Who-ee. Broke my jaws. Cousin, think she said. Boy, I've got to go lie down."

Jim moved over, staring at the back of Effie's head. "Here."

"Jim, you know I can't sleep out here. My dress hiking up, people passing—"

"Helen Taylor's cousin passed by. What did *she* see."

"Him. I said it was a boy." He was freed. He let Effie pass on into the house.

He thought she was taking his sleep with her, but almost immediately drowsiness came to hover over him, casting a shadow, and he had to, or wanted to, with his last energy, turn over on his stomach. In his dream he did it without having to wear Short Pecker, but who it was who was taking him he could not see. All he knew was that the person receiving him loved his bigness and told him so, over and over, and said other words that drew his sweat in deep rivers.

He awoke with the sure feeling that he was watched. He looked first to the road—Effie's training—that he shared with his neighbor, Barnes. A cloud of dust hung at the bend, but it was moving toward him. Barnes, on his way back to the fields, could not have seen him over the sumac. He looked to the house. He was still half in his dream; if he had seen someone without a face it would not have startled him, but there was no one. The shades were drawn at the bedroom windows, so it had not been Effie watching him from the bed in fear as he humped the ground. When Barnes came into view Jim got up and entered the house.

23

He tiptoed through the parlor and went into the bedroom. Watching Effie closely for signs of waking, he opened his dresser drawer and felt for a clean jock strap. His hand encountered Short Pecker, and he took the device out and grinned at it, feeling sheepish.

Just then he heard Barnes say "Hidy," not shouting at the house as he sometimes did but in a conversational tone that carried through the still air. Jim pulled aside the shade and stared out, straining his eyes for whoever Barnes had spoken to, but all that occupied the silence was the cloud of dust hanging over Barnes like an umbrella, and the ring of the mare's shoe striking a rock.

When he turned back into the room Effie was staring not at him but at the brutal limiting device in his hand.

"No," she said, sliding off the bed sideways like a crab, "you've already—"

He relaxed, not hating her expression, not wanting to crack her jaw. She *had* been the one who watched him.

"Suppose," he said, "that wasn't enough for a grown-up hot-blooded man." He grinned to see her anger break, sensing the huge relief in it.

"Jim Cummins, you're a goddamned disgrace and that's the truth. You know dadburn well I can't help it if you're—if I'm—" Jim turned it into a joke, though not without a cutting edge, by saying, "Don't take on, string bean. Nobody's blaming you. A man needs a change, is all." He leered at her. "Pretty good piece of ground we got out there."

She turned, really mad, and tore out of the room, her hands plucking at her apron strings as if she was going to take the thing off and go somewhere, anywhere away from him. It was her greatest gesture of frustration, tearing at her apron strings that way. Jim knew she would not actually take it off, which would be like taking off her daytime skin, but would stop in the middle of the next room and stand there, head down, mouth slacked open, while her fingers plucking at the knot gave smaller and smaller pinches until they stopped and hooked over the strings, and then her hands would fall to her sides and she would be over her temper.

He had seen the same performance time without number in nine years of marriage, but never before because of sex. He wondered, putting on clean cool jeans, if she had some secret too, some memory, like his of Ludie, and if something had happened today to stir it up. It puzzled him to think that there might be things about Effie that he did not know, had not suspected, and he was tentative with her when he went into the room where she stood, as he knew she would be, with head tucked down, hands falling loose at her sides.

"Good news about Junie," he said, and she nodded, resigned, before she lifted her head and pride over her sister's catch brought some life back into her face. Then, as though it were a duty, she touched his arm and said, "I wasn't spying on you, Jim. I was just drifting off when I heard something—somebody. I thought it was you. Footsteps. You can hear a cat walk on that dried-up old grass. Dream, I guess. Guess I had drifted off and didn't know it. But when I got up and looked—"

At the supper table, over the blackberry cobbler left untouched at dinnertime, Effie said, "I declare if I don't beat all." She pushed back her chair and her hands rose and fell to her lap. It was a gesture inherited from her mother to express almost all moods and emotions except mourning and passion, in whose territories she was left on her own because, according to Jim's observations, those were two places the old lady had never been. Effie's gesture and words, as used currently, could be read to mean that she had forgot to serve relish with the cold meat, or to answer her mother's letter. Drama accompanied small things for Effie, but he imagined she would kill quietly and coldly.

"How's that, string bean?" Jim was relaxed enough to feel indulgent. The radio had reported rain upstate, the war news was favorable—no local boys reported dead or missing—and he had finished suckering the tobacco which that morning he had calculated would take him at least part of the following day. His ability to lose himself in what he was doing was an acquired skill that was not always dependable, but desire to succeed, plus necessity to forget all of what had happened at noon, especially his thoughts about Ludie, had helped him to a state of mindlessness. He had been propelled up and down the rows like a machine, troubles and memories buried under layers of work and sweat, the two things he could believe in because they never deserted him.

It had been close to eight o'clock when he turned to start down the next row and found himself trying to sucker barbed wire. Effie must have been joined to him in spirit, for when he got to the house, cows had been milked, hogs slopped, horses watered and fed, chickens put to roost. She had also pushed the hand plow up and down the rows of the vegetable garden and gathered what she could of its fruit for canning tomorrow. At times like these, not too infrequent, Jim was a contented man. That a necessary feature of his content was bone-weariness, which canceled out thoughts of sex, was something he accepted each time at the time, without learning from it. He could not pretend indifference to his rights any more than he could find a way, when he had to give in and exercise those rights, to spare Effie pain. If the doctor couldn't —and though Short Pecker worked to a degree, sometimes Jim got carried away and Effie screamed—Jim couldn't.

Effie, knowing herself safe for the night, used her body freely to illustrate why she "beat all." Standing up, hand on chest, hand on hip, foot propped on chair rung, she declaimed.

"I'm falling apart, that's all! I promised Helentaylor. Said I'd keep a lookout, case she didn't get a ride out 'til late. Said I'd *feed* the boy. Promised I'd walk over and fetch him back for supper if she didn't send word! And here it is quarter to nine—" Reaching for the apron strings: "Junie's wedding, and the chores—it went clean out of my mind. I'd better get over there. You go on to bed." Her hands were torn between apron strings and dishes of food; he saw it as a battle between vanity and charity, and it was an old voice in his head pointing out various ways to look at familiar things. "Yes, Miss Ethel," he said and grinned to see Effie take no notice at having been transformed into his old teacher.

"Lord, I can't just take him leftover supper like a dog!"

"We dogs?"

"Scraps, from dinnertime."

"That's what we had."

"Aw, Jim, they weren't scraps when we sat down to the table."

"She probably got a ride around to the other road."

"Who lives back there, would be coming home so late. I don't know a soul back there's got priority, nor an automobile to put the gasoline in 'cept Johnson's Model T and the boys all off in the War. *He* can't drive it, drawn up like a knot, last time I saw him. Hate to think of him trying and Helentaylor in there with him."

"I don't know why she keeps working in town with no way to get in and out."

"Now, Jim. Out, just out. There's the milk truck in the mornings." No kidding, he thought, thinking of the time wasted in the barn each morning waiting for Helen Taylor to finish her coffee with Effie and get on the truck and go.

"And what'd she do for a living, I ask you? Now, if she had the place rent free—" He would be damned if he would give her the place, house and five acres, rent free. Effie never could let go, but a fat lot of good it would do her. He got up, his good mood going, and started for the bedroom.

"Take a lantern. There's no moon tonight."

"Jim, if you would—"

"I'm not going to."

"If you would she could make five dollars a week at the store in Salvation. Huffines offered that much and no more. Vinnie gone off again and Rosy sick, you'd think it'd be worth more, but no, he'd rather hang on to his dollars, 'til a heart attack puts him out of commission for good. Then we'll see what happens to the store. Vinnie'd come back and sell it to the first bidder and take off forever. Still, if Helentaylor had five dollars a week and *time*, she could raise a big enough garden to still come out on top."

"She can have a garden now. Her kin can take care of it."

"He's sickly, I think." Effie was suddenly vague. "Something or other she said makes me think— Oh." She sounded odd, and Jim turned around, but she was all over the place, gathering together an egg basket from the back porch and a clean dish towel from the kitchen cupboard, putting food on saucers and pouring milk into a jug. He watched her awhile, puzzling over what he thought he had heard in a syllable, and from the way she did not inquire why he was standing there staring, he thought he had been right: that she was hiding something, though he could not imagine what it could be. Sickly, she said. What could be bad enough to make her sound that way and stop like that? T.b.? He thought he had heard about a kind that was catching, but he would not place himself at her mercy by asking.

"Him probably lying over there with his feet sticking up, poor little feller." Jim accepted the explanation and felt relieved. Effie had been recalled from her missionary work of trying to squeeze a donation out of him for her favorite charity, Helen Taylor, to thoughts about the hungry boy. He was grateful to the boy, whoever he was, and whatever he had, or had had, to make him sickly. He went in the bedroom and took off his shirt and shoes and pants. Effie came to the door and said, "I might stay awhile—" like a question. Jim mumbled, and she left.

Jim took off his socks and lay back on the bed in his jock strap. In spite of pushing himself extra hard at suckering the tobacco he was not as tired or sleepy as he had thought. He forced yawns until his ears popped, with the result that he was wider awake than ever. Whatever sleep there was in him seemed to have gone out into the room on the expelled breaths of yawns. He gazed around at things made half familiar by the seeping light from the kitchen. Ashamed and amused to involve her, he invited Miss Ethel back into his head, asking her if she had ever wondered about him under his clothes, asking how she would have him view the big mound of himself in the jock strap, bordered by the fringe of coarse curling hair. As though she had replied, he saw it as the bandaged head of a soldier.

He thought with bitterness that it might as well be in a sling. It sure as hell had to walk with a crutch when it walked at all. Without Short Pecker his wife would die like a stuck pig, or split open like a watermelon with a stob through it. Since his wedding night, even in his wet dreams he wore the thing. In his waking hours, when he thought about it, it was as if part of his flesh and blood was kept in a dresser drawer. He felt crippled with it and crippled without it. He would never know if it would have made a difference if he had married Ludie, whether or not Effie's smallness was at least partly to blame. He had come to think of himself, a great part of the time, as a brute, a near monster without his clothes, but a small corner of doubt remained because he could not accept the idea of himself as a total victim and stay a sane man. His most effective strategy was to think as little as possible, and it was these efforts all afternoon and into evening that were responsible for Miss Ethel's presence in his head. She had helped him to learn to think, through conversation, recommended reading, special interest, explaining herself as "that cliché, a teacher looking for *just one pupil—*" which she had thought to have found in him. Once in his drunk days, staggering around the daytime streets of town, he ran into her. When she tried to pass by with a nod he held her, insisting that he was looking for the library. "Why, yonder it is, Jim," she said and pointed to the saloon. He let her go then. They were two failures dismissing each other.

For since school days he had discovered that his thoughts, if let free for a time without restraints, could astound and dismay him. There would be bitterness afterward when he had to squeeze his mind away again. He had arrived at an equation: total freedom of thought equaled discontent and pain. And there was a hangover, worse than the morning after liquor, that shredded his temper and made him snap at human and beast alike. Thus he taught himself, counter to her teaching, to achieve mindlessness in work. This had been his answer to the problem of alcoholism, too, for he had been a thoughtful drunk, his philosophizing a source of high mirth to his companions.

But he could not work every minute of his life, and so the old danger waited for him, catching him, as tonight, before sleep. He started to get up and go to the kitchen and stuff himself, which was another way to control his thoughts. Sitting on the edge of the bed he remembered that Effie had taken all the food to feed the strange kid. He lay back and tried simply imagining the rain falling upstate and moving down, taking a county at a time, heavy and black as a camouflaged maneuvering army in the night, the Allies to the rescue of all the little people left behind, burned out by the enemy, the sun.

He recalled floodwaters he had seen, the great flood of '37, when he was twenty and two years married, and remembered the helplessness and his hate for the rain as he watched his land disappear a field at a time under the muddy almost blood-red water. One was as bad as the other, the rain and the sun, once the scale slipped out of balance. There were people to whom the Allies were the enemy. Not just Hitler and Tojo and their armies, but the little people caught in between, the way his farm had been caught between the high ground and the river. And yet those same little people had victims of their own, or they wouldn't be human.

In anger he threshed the bed and beat the pillow. What was the good of working yourself like a mule if you couldn't sleep at the end of it! He could have smacked Effie for going off into the night. He had a strong urge to go out to the barn, but he had never given in at night ever before, and he would not start now. Some things that were natural under certain circumstances could become unnatural under others; he told himself he could not afford to risk ruining a "good" thing. He saw the word in quotes. Miss Ethel had talked that way, managing to say whatever she really thought about the rest of the faculty by putting the "good" words in quotes. Jim had picked it up as a thought habit, a "sophistication," another of Miss Ethel's words. He wondered if there was such a thing as something being really "good," or if everything in the world—causes, people, weather—were just degrees of "bad." Effie gone off to feed a hungry kid—that was surely good. But the place she went to was bad to him, because Ludie had lived in that house and gone crazy there: his tenant house, where she had come to stay with her kin, Mrs. Helen Taylor, and met him and lost all she had.

His mental violence reached out for Junie, Effie's whorey sister, whose coming wedding he thought was responsible for Ludie being so much, so desperately, on his mind. She lived there like a natural cell, but today she was trying to burst out on a hemorrhage, freeing herself and killing him. He wished that he could die for her, and now.

Sweat was running down his face, getting in his ears, and the hairs under his arms seemed to be filled sponges. Willfully he conjured the flood waters of '37, imagining that he could hear the cold waters slapping at the steps of the front porch. The wagon road did not exist; no vehicle could carry any-body out through that red lake. "A hearse-boat," he said, and though he had never seen a horse-drawn hearse he had the image of black-plumed horses swimming by, water shooting from their nostrils, and he answered brutally, "No. A crazy girl could have turned a boat over," and watched the horses go under. They had been trying to take Ludie away, and they had not made it.

During the flood of '37 people had been pushed from the bottomlands along the river in herds to higher ground, to ask for food and shelter at the farms and houses around Salvation, a bluff community. Some of them had been quar-tered in the church and schoolhouse; others made do with lean-tos built out of any and everything and begged for their food, or snitched it when they could find a chance. Nobody but old Huffines at the store ever used a stronger word for it than "snitch." Old Huffines said "stole" and swore he would get every penny back somehow. His prices bore him out.

One day Jim went to the store for something—news, prob-ably; his battery radio went dead sometime late in the crisis. He rowed himself out to the main road in a barn-built boat and walked the three miles to the store. There was only a slight drizzle falling then, but water lapped at his shoes when-ever he strayed away from the white line down the center of the high road. When he got to the store there was a crowd milling around on the store porch, some of them eating cheese and crackers and candy bars and some not. Some watched. There was a woman, skinny as a rail—her cheekbones stuck out like doorknobs; Jim imagined that if you touched one her face would open up—and a kid, about five, who looked like his bones were laid on top of what flesh he had. They were mother and son, you could tell by the eyes, but the woman circled one way and the kid another, just looking, but asking plainer than words. Every now and then she would check on him and then circle some more. Most of the people were refugees, most of them men, and the ones that were eating turned like weathervanes to keep their backs to the woman and the boy.

Jim watched for a while, because it was his habit, and then went in the store and bought a box of crackers, a pound of cheese, four or five candy bars, and two Dr. Peppers. He spent all the money he had on him. He went back outside and set the kid up on the top of a gas pump and hand-fed him, cramming the stuff in his mouth because people were gathering around to watch and Jim was embarrassed. He did not look around to see if the mother was one of the watchers; he meant to feed the boy first, all it could hold, and give the rest to her. Jim pushed rat cheese and saltines and Clark Bar into the kid and poured Dr. Pepper down him.

The kid started throwing up all at once, and Jim jumped back out of the way. He was almost knocked down by the mother rushing to the boy. She clamped her hand over its mouth, trying to hold the food in. Vomit spewed around and between her fingers. She jerked her son down from the pump and held him pressed against her legs with her hand over his mouth. Her shoulders were bent over and shaking. Jim could not see her face but he did not think she was crying. It was more as if the shaking was caused by nerves, or anxiousness. The puke kept coming; when she saw that she could not make the boy keep the nourishment down, she cupped her hands under his chin and caught the stuff in them and lifted the cup to her mouth and ate, or drank.

Jim put what was left of the food he bought on the top of

the gas pump and started to walk away, but before he had turned completely around to head off home one of the refugees grabbed the cheese and started eating it from one hand while the other was stuffing crackers and candy bars in the pockets of his overalls. When Jim left, the woman was fighting the man for the food and had got two of the candy bars away from him. No word was said, by the woman or the man or the watchers. The only sound was of the kid heaving up the last of what Jim had fed him, as though charity had frozen closed the road to his stomach.

Jim turned over onto his belly, pressing hard against the bed, hoping pressure would cut off the source of his anxiety and keep it from reaching his brain. Eventually the picture of the starving boy, whom his compassion had hurt, merged with the picture, faceless except for a mouth, of the boy being fed by Effie. As Jim fell asleep the image became as fluid as water. Now it was the teenage figure he had seen at the gate that morning, and now it was a baby suckling at Effie's miraculously rounded, full breast.

II

Jim woke up before the rooster crowed and lay savoring with all his body the cool stream of air that moved through the open kitchen door, through the bedroom across his and Effie's bodies, and out of the front windows under partly raised shades. No matter how hot the days became, or how long the heat and drought continued, the low—in normal weather, marshy—land behind his barns drew up from itself during the night a coolness that could carry an edge of chill. This coolness was pulled toward the hills in front of the house where the sun would rise, passing through the house on its way. In summertime the bed was kept angled out in the middle of the floor, to lie in the path of the morning air. Everyone else that Jim knew slept during the hottest weather on pallets beneath windows or under mosquito netting on porches, but Jim's great-grandfather, who built the house, had designed it to take full advantage of what was a peculiarity of his land.

The house was in three flat low-ceilinged layers like a squashed cake. It was narrow, its long sides facing east and west. The gallerylike many-windowed kitchen ran half the length of the house, then joined onto a series of well-insulated darkish storage rooms, which shared a common wall with the parlor and into which one of the three fireplaces was built. From the kitchen you reached the dining room and bedroom downstairs, or mounted by closed staircase to the big right-angled hall and four bedrooms, thence to the huge only partially finished attic—two completed chambers and a dim expanse of rafters and catwalked joists. It was possible, by a judicious arrangement of furniture, to enjoy in all the rooms except the upstairs northeast and northwest bedrooms the natural air-conditioning which Jim's ancestor had considered part of God's bounty. Those two cut-off rooms had once benefited from his ancestor's planning, too, but the connecting door between them had been locked by Jim's great-grand-mother and the key thrown away. Since that day it had not seriously occurred to anyone to alter the arrangement.

When Jim's great-grandparents had had only one son, in-stead of the three they had planned for, his great-grand-mother had claimed the two connecting rooms for her own and had made them into winter and summer sitting rooms, interchangeable, to catch or avoid the sun as it struck her mood. She had loathed drafts—her word for even the gentle current in which Jim now lay—and had precluded the possi-bility of one entering either of her sitting rooms by locking the door between and disposing of the key. From Jim's grand-father's time until Jim's adult life, the bedrooms had been kept filled with children, adults, old people. Not until Jim's tenure as owner following the death of his mother had the upstairs lain empty and silent. Now the only traffic on the stairs would be Effie transporting canned stuffs to their caches in the closets (the storage rooms downstairs having been trans-formed into modern utility rooms) or by Jim going to the attic to check and repair leakholes.

When Jim first brought Effie to the house as his bride, after a three-day honeymoon at the Moonbow Lodge in the Cum-berlands, they had, over his mother's feeble protests, occupied the big bedroom upstairs. They had shared the floor with Jim's sister, Clara, whose northeast room was separated from theirs by the "bath," a primitive ancestor of the modern bath-room downstairs; it contained a tub to which water had to be carried, and a chamber pot concealed in a piece of furniture like a tall chair. The room had been the talk of the surround-ing farms and had earned for Jim's great-grandmother the epithet of "spoiled." Will, Jim and Clara's younger brother, spent all of his spare time in the northwest bedroom, separated from his sister by more than the locked door in between, and from Jim by a greater distance than the hall.

Clara was engaged to a Northerner, Jim was married, and

Will, who was fifteen when Jim brought Effie home, was dedicated to an ideal that was finding disciples in Europe, and worshiped the idealist who originated the new religion, Naziism.

No one in the house knew more at the time than that Will was quiet, and secretive about his mail, some of which came from far-off places. His death in Germany, in 1937, when he was seventeen, was practically the beginning as well as the end of their knowledge of his secret life. He had left in the winter of 1936, conscientiously waiting until the work was light, ostensibly to travel through the Southwestern states with penpals. Now, six years after his death, Jim knew little more than that he had died in a country that was the enemy. The letter that notified them of Will's death had called him a "hero" but had not explained why this was so, nor had it specified how he died.

A picture of Hitler, cut from a magazine, was found in his closet, along with a snapshot of Hans Mueller's daughter, with whom he had gone to school. The photograph of the plump blonde girl was caked with a dried substance which could have been glue, or mucus. Jim's mother had found the photograph and called for him. Laughing and weeping at the same time, she said, "If he loved the Germans so much why did he blow his nose on Mattie Mae's picture!" Jim knew what the substance was, but he did not know how to fit it into the rest of the puzzle of his brother.

Jim seldom thought about Will. It was as if most of the time, he had never existed. He thought about him this morning because of the young boy who seemed to have occupied so much of yesterday—of Effie's time and, in retrospect, of his emotions, because he felt that seeing the boy looking at him from the gate at dinnertime, where Ludie used to stand and wave while he worked, could account for a great deal of his morbidity and even for his wet dream.

He wondered if his feeling of being watched when he awoke from the dream was because he had been, by the boy sneaking around. He changed that to "walking around." But Woody Barnes had spoken to someone. At least he spoke. For that matter he could have said "Giddy-up" to the mare.

Jim thought to hell with it. He stretched cautiously so as not to wake Effie. He would get up and light the coal-oil stove in a minute and put the coffee on. He was reluctant to leave the cool bed and the peaceful gray light of the bedroom, which he could imagine, while he lay there, came from a soft, full cover of clouds. Once he got up and saw the streakless white sky from the kitchen windows the fact of the drought could not be put off any longer. Now, here, the odors from the barn riding in on the airflow smelled damp and rich, as if a steady rain had stirred up the manure and corncobs and trampled hay until they were as aromatic and good to his nose as the potpourri Effie made out of dried flowers and herbs, the way his mother had taught her. Her own mother had not known any such recipes to hand on because the only smell she knew, to acknowledge, was the smell of money.

Jim had never had a pleasant thought about Effie's mother and never would, but this morning, to his surprise, he found himself regretting the intrusion of such a sour note, and then realized why. Days that began as this one had, with thoughts of family history as represented and contained by the house, usually were good days. It was always at this point, after the thoughts had been thought, that he recognized such days, saw the omens, felt the results. He seemed to be bound more firmly to his place, and by the reminder that he had a history, and that history went forward as well as stretched back, he felt his aims renewed to fulfill his part as well and honorably as he could.

On one such morning it had occurred to him that it was like drinking from a wellspring in the woods, come upon suddenly when he was hot and tired and had lost the path, which had become overgrown from not being used. He had liked the idea and told himself that he would mark the spring so that he could find it again when he needed it, but he had later discovered that when he deliberately sought it out, it was not as refreshing to him. In puzzling about it he had concluded that surprise and relief must have some kind of connection and tried to find out, in a roundabout way, by consulting Effie and Woody Barnes, if he had made a discovery about people. It was an old ambition, to be the first to point out something to people that might benefit them. When he was hot and thirsty, he told them, he knew just how far he would have to go to get a drink and how long it would take him to get there, and so he wondered if knowing this half satisfied his thirst before he ever got to the water, and whether that would make the relief only half as great? Woody said, naw, he reckoned not; when he was thirsty, he was *thirsty*. He seemed put out by the question. Effie laughed and asked Jim if he was "studying to be a psychologer." He felt curiously lonely for their rejection, as though for a moment he had woven into their common past similar conversations, when Miss Ethel, and in a different way, Ludie, had been the only ones ever to encourage him to think and talk as anything but "a good old boy." It was the one time he had ventured to show his underside (like a snake, he thought ironically) to his good neighbor and his life's companion and had learned from the mistake. Both Woody and Effie studied him for a time afterward, speculating upon him as though he were a stranger, but in due course the episode was forgotten.

This morning, recalling the spring, Jim thought that Will's fate was because he had not believed himself to have such a spring to visit and drink from. Which edged on Jim's thoughts of last night concerning victims, and he set it aside for some other time.

He thought instead about the boy who had brought Will to mind, but this time he did not feel resentment and not too much interest. He could not very well resent the boy as a trespasser when he was not. As a tenant he was entitled to the run of the place just as the Negroes had been. And he was no longer of particular interest because Jim knew that he would hear all about the kid from Effie at breakfast, so that his curiosity, like his theoretical thirst, was already half satisfied by the knowledge. Effie's "I might stay awhile" when she left last night had not been due to a special need, tired as she was, to visit with Helen Taylor, someone she saw at least once a day during the work week and more often on week ends, but by a tireless interest in any new person who might come along, regardless of age, color, or sex. Thinking about it that way, he commiserated with her: it was a lonesome old life, all right. Effie went along from day to day, doing what she had to do, maybe for stretches of time not noticing her lonesomeness, or turning on the radio for company when she did, but let somebody new come along and all her banked-up needs burst out like fire through ashes. The only reason she had not had the boy with her in the house all day yesterday, pumping him for news about the part of the country he came from, was because he had been overshadowed by the only thing that could overshadow a stranger: news of Effie's own family. She waited for her mother's infrequent letters the way Jim waited for rain.

Which led Jim to the edge of his own loneliness, a sure sign that it was time for him to get up. If the day came when all a farmer had to do was loll in bed, missing his black field hands! Which was part of the truth but hardly all of it.

He got out of bed, and as he dressed he let the rest come. It was about his son as yet unsired. It usually contained some pain, but this morning, for a reason beyond him, it presented itself positively for his inspection like a child who knows its hands and ears are clean. Jim looked at Effie balled up under the sheet, no bigger than a kid herself, and thought, "Both of us twenty-seven; healthy; there's time."

He set the alarm to go off in fifteen minutes, went into the kitchen and lit the stove and put the coffee on. He took milk buckets from their nails on the screened-in back porch, his addition, along with the now useless bathroom off the kitchen, to his great-grandfather's basic design. Except in times of severe drought, when they had to go back to using the privy and chamber pots and dishpans, Effie had a house as convenient as any in town. His mother had not had running water in the house until Jim put in the pipes himself, going by a booklet put out by the State, after his father died.

His father had believed that having water so easily available would lead to waste, which would drain the wells in no time. Jim thought that about summed up his father, without unfairness, putting into a nutshell his attitude to life: that enjoyment and appreciation came from hard work, and that too much convenience made waste. By that yardstick, Jim's father had led a life of enjoyment and appreciation and not too much waste. He died in 1930 when Jim was thirteen and too young, or too callow, to have noticed whether or not his father was happy, but Jim remembered him with affection as a cheerful, opinionated man who was still spoken about in Salvation as if he were alive. Somebody would begin a story about his father: "Old Tom, there—" the man would say, and nod in the direction of the graveyard behind the church as if Old Tom had just wandered back there to the privy and would be coming out any minute.

Because of their father, both Will and Jim had been given the benefit of doubts when their actions might otherwise have led to censure: Jim, when he was sowing his wild oats in an alcoholic binge that lasted almost the entire first year of his marriage, was excused thus: "Boy wakes up and finds he's hogtied at eighteen, he's going to behave like a hog. He'll pull out of it. He's Old Tom's boy." And Will, when word got around about his death in Germany, was understood through his father: "Old Tom thought a lot of his German neighbors. Helped them whenever they needed it. Was his boy going to be different?"

When America entered the War, the German neighbors—Schmidts, Weidermanns, Fehrles—who had relatives fighting on the other side, were boycotted and were not allowed to trade at the store in Salvation, but Old Tom's boy, Will, wasn't mentioned any longer. As far as they were concerned, Old Tom had one son, the spit and image of his dad, who took after his dad in all the ways that counted to them. When their sons enlisted, or were drafted, they held no grudges against Jim, who was handed deferment after deferment. They said if he had his way, he'd be in there killing Germans alongside the rest.

And yet at times, especially those times of his melancholy, Jim thought that out of all the people who slapped him on the back and called him "Old Buddy" at the store or at events at the schoolhouse (Jim and Effie were not churchgoers), not one was a friend earned by his own efforts, nor had their efforts earned his regard. They had inherited each other from his father.

He thought this was truer than ever now that most of the young men had left; anyway, a lot of them had only been drinking buddies, and when he gave it up and settled down, they had drifted on to others as restless as they were, looking for safety from the very thing Jim was already committed to when he was one of them. The War had been their final answer, and they had enlisted together, drunk and triumphant, leaving the girls they had used—girls like Junie—to find husbands among the elderly widowers and old bachelors who had stayed that way because no girl would have them. Though in Junie's case it was the other way around, if reputation counted.

Beginning to milk the first heifer, he pressed his head against her side and told her, "Junie's lucky she found anybody. I'm telling you, that girl was more than a pushover. She grabbed me more than once."

The last time Jim had not pushed her away, curious to see her reaction to nature taking its full course. "Ohhhhhh" she had gone, her little eyes wide, but when he kept growing she had snatched her hand away as if a fire had burned it. By that, heated as he was and despairing, Jim figured that Effie had not told her sister about the cross she had to bear. She obviously had kept as quiet about it as if he were a nigger under his clothes.

He told the other heifers, as he caressed the milk from their udders, that Old Man Dobbs, Junie's intended, was getting himself a bride who had put out for six young men in one night, and according to their story she had begged for more. If a girl could take all that and not be satisfied, and yet backed away from him, he concluded—an initial conclusion leading to still another—that he belonged right where he was, in the barn with the other animals.

The heifers were familiar with Junie's story, and others of similar content, all involving hot insatiable girls. They were familiar with the stories' progression, and the inevitable outcome when the narrator justified animal behavior by practicing it. The growing agitation of the hands which furnished them relief was familiar, and the eventual transfer of the hands to the body of their owner, to the ultimate relief of the owner's body. Nothing in the ritual startled the cows. It was part of the comfortable beginning of many of their days. The only difference between their relief and his was Jim's peculiar feeling of pride afterward. The core of it was that he had confined his indulgence to the barn. The marriage bed, such as it was, belonged to Effie, and even when he took her against her will, which was nearly always, he tried to think thoughts that would not have offended her if she had known them. But in the barn he was his own man, and if the body was truly vile, he could revel in it, for he was not a man of half measures. And thinking that always amused him; it was his favorite joke on himself. In the barn, bitterness was given no quarter.

Perhaps his father had been like him, but instead of giving in he had fought it. Why else had he dinned into his boys that part of the Bible about not spilling seed on the ground, and others that had to do with man's base impulses? When Jim discovered his base and viewed it in the light of his father's sermons, he had stopped going to church.

And Will. The picture. The plump German girl. Covered with mucus. Caked around her mouth.

Leaving the stall, buttoning up his jeans, Jim thought with deliberate raucous humor that Will hadn't needed to go to Germany to die, if he did it because of sex. He could have stayed at home and married Junie and died a piece at a time, or somebody like Effie and died by his own hand!

He spilled a little milk from one of the pails into a cupped hand and washed himself.

He carried the milk into the tack room and poured it in with last night's through the strainer into the big cans which were packed down in a box with sawdust and pond ice from his own icehouse and covered with damp feed sacks. He turned the livestock out, all but one mule which he hitched to the sledge to draw the milk cans to the front of the house beside the mailbox where the truck would pick them up. He loaded the cans onto the sledge and tapped the mule on the rump, then pulled back and stood listening. He had been so caught up in his thoughts that he wondered if he had missed it, but before long he heard Helen Taylor humming up the wagon road. When she passed the barn the humming grew in volume, so much so that her voice cracked a little. Jim had always used the humming as a signal to wait for her to get by, but today he wondered if she actually meant it that way, if it was not a warning to him that she would soon be in his kitchen drinking coffee and to lay low until she was gone. There was certainly no love lost between them, though they always managed to be civil to each other for Effie's sake, when they were thrown together. But the idea that she might want to avoid him to the extent of warning him did not sit too well. He liked to be the one to make decisions concerning himself. If there was punishment to follow, he would decide whether or not to take it. He wondered why the idea of Helen Taylor's warning him had waited so many years to crop up. He felt literally lightheaded, as if too much light had entered his head and was blinding him from within.

Feeling halfway to temper, he drove the mule out of the barn and rode the sledge down the incline to the wagon road, adding his weight for balance, then got off and walked.

If he ignored Helen Taylor's warning and went into the kitchen early while she was still there, what could he be punished with? He knew damned well: the possibility was always with him, sometimes submerged, that she could tell Effie about Ludie. Incredible as it was, Effie knew nothing about Ludie. The gossip had not reached her part of the country before they were married, he supposed as the result of complicity between his and Effie's mothers, who had somehow bribed or threatened Helen Taylor into silence. Now she was forced to keep his secret because of knowing which side her bread was buttered on. Jim only charged her ten dollars a month rent for the house and five acres. She'd have to pay that much a week for a room in town. Jim could not imagine her telling Effie unless—unless what? Ah. He began to see a pattern in Effie's repeated attempts to get him to give Helen Taylor the place rent free. He saw now that the idea had not originated with Effie.

He felt a chill which he tried to beat off by swinging the

cans with great force onto the concrete. The last can, half empty, rang like a dinner bell. He straightened up and looked around for possible witnesses, feeling on guard. Straight ahead, over the hills, the white curve of the sun, almost the same color as the sky, looked like the bald head of an old sick man lifting from a white pillow. A semicircle of trees in silhouette against it and to the sides seemed to be waiting, like gathered kin, for it to die. Jim was simultaneously racked by loneliness and a feeling that he was not alone, and the contradiction—bitter, and too sweet—resolved itself into a taste in his mouth; it was as though he had drunk from a cup of coffee that he had thought was black, and discovered that it had been sugared. It was as though he drank from another's cup, and his first, ingrained impulse was to hawk and spit, but the sweet aftertaste was oddly pleasant on his tongue. The hallucinations vanished before the reality of his stomach rumbling, and he found himself, vacant-eyed and empty-minded, staring directly into the sun.

After a moment the idea of Helen Taylor's warning sifted back into his consciousness, but his anger had been sieved out; he could only vaguely recall it, like something of no importance that happened last week. It was replaced by an awareness of her as a woman who was getting on in years; she was probably fifty; and a certain wary tenderness invaded him. He thought about her walking up the road in the summer dawns and the dark of winter, humming to keep up her spirits. Because she spent most of her time in town, he had always thought of her as a town woman, but now he would bet that she would gladly exchange her job as waitress for the hard work of a farmer's wife. She probably envied Effie her chances to nap, to take off her shoes, to listen to the radio. She had nothing of her own, nobody; the "Mrs." in front of her name was the camouflage of many a woman passed over by life. Something in Jim's light-filled head said clearly, "She has a son, now."

He clucked to the mule, and they started back. Jim stared down at the road whose normally sharp ruts had been ground down by drought and daily passage until they were hardly more prominent than the ridges on a washboard, and were almost obscured by dust as fine as baby powder, which spurted in little puffs under his and the mule's feet. The unburdened sledge rode the dust as smoothly as if it floated on water. The mule nodded as though in agreement, or to sport the black plume it wore.

To get rid of the image, he made a picture of himself appearing in the kitchen where the two women were having coffee. He would behave as naturally as could be, but the act itself should let Helen Taylor know that she did not have to think he was hiding from her any more. Nine years, he would tell her silently, is enough.

Anticipating the look on their two faces—Effie's pleased, Helen Taylor's startled but open—he grinned. He whacked the mule, and when it took off at a smart clip, causing the sledge to buck and veer, Jim jumped aboard and stood widelegged, shifting his weight from foot to foot, feeling as exhilarated as if the unsettled dust were waterspray on his face. If Helen Taylor was willing to let bygones go, then so was he!

He stood outside the screen door tuning up. "Well, well," he said in his mind, heard his feet clomping across the porch and the slam of the door, saw himself enter the kitchen rubbing his hands, and the two lighted-up, surprised, and pleased faces turned to him. It was so easy to give pleasure—that was one to write down in the permanent book. A man kept learning, and it seemed like the simple things took longest. Came hardest, too: the hand he put out for the doorknob was trembling, and the arm was weak. Sitting on that arm were nine years, like nine heavy birds—nine, the heaviest of the single numbers, which required two trips of the tongue to the roof of the mouth to say it. And yet to carry out his plan he had to be light, breezy, natural as daylight.

"Well, well," he said, booming, going onto the porch, but the tight spring of the door slammed it shut on his second "well." He wondered how his one audible "well" sounded to the women in the kitchen. Not generous, maybe even unpleasant. One "well" was what you said when you were taken off guard. If he added another "well" now it would sound even worse—"Well" SLAM "well"—as if he were emphasizing his displeasure at finding Helen Taylor still there. No, it would be worse still: "Well SLAM—pause—well"—that was downright ominous. All a man could do after that was turn and go.

It was getting out of hand, he could tell by the shocked silence that was like something electric standing in the kitchen door. The faces that he had imagined as lighted up, surprised, and pleased, he could see clearly in his mind's eye as they stared at the empty doorway like two rabbits cornered by weasels. Lettuce leaves, half chewed, hung from their mouths, and their noses twitched. His loathing at having been turned into a beast bared his teeth and sent him into a mental half crouch. He was so feral he could smell himself. Imagining their terror at the sight of him entering the kitchen apelike was so pleasing that he translated the image into action. He was swinging his arms, getting the rhythm, when behind him Effiie said, "What on earth—" He wheeled, scraping his nose on the screen and banging his head on a two-by-four.

Effie's bright eyes bored into his cage, curiously compassionate. The bunch of parsley in her hand completed his downfall. He howled in anger and pain at the blow to his head and his scraped nose. She came swiftly through the door and reached up and touched his head where the lump was rapidly rising.

"Why, honey," she said, and the extreme rarity of the endearment brought him to himself. She only used it when he was sick or otherwise entirely helpless, which was hardly ever. He was neither of those things now. He gave her hand a pat, pushing it away at the same time, and preceded her into the kitchen. Helen Taylor's cup was washed and drying on the drainboard. Bacon shriveled on a piece of brown paper bag. Eggs for scrambling were broken in a bowl. What had happened was plain: the milk truck had come and gone without his hearing. Effie had been on her way to call him to breakfast—

"I was on my way to call you. What took you so—"

He overlapped her, confident and easy and natural as daylight.

"Banged my hand. Soaked it in the barn. Was looking at it to see—"

"—when I made you bang your head!" They nodded to each other, all mystery cleared away. "Well, you did look funny, 'sall I can say! Like you were about to—I don't know—*spring*—"

She scurried around, beating eggs, heating fat, peeping at the biscuits in the oven.

"Do you want me to get some blackberry jam from the cellar?"

"Uh uh."

"Well, I didn't think you'd want it, 'swhy I just put out the peach. After the cobbler last night, I thought you'd had enough blackberries for a while." Jim nodded patiently. She always fussed over the food, offering explanations for why everything in the house wasn't on the table at one time.

"There's just bacon," she said obviously, "but if you wanted some ham I could—" glancing at him. He shook his head. She clarified her position on the matter of ham. "Seems to me like ham is just too heavy for weather as hot and dry as this. And so salty. Of course, we need salt in hot weather. My daddy always drank a cup of hot salt water on summer mornings before he'd touched his coffee. And plain hot water in the wintertime. Now, why did he put a slice of lemon in that plain hot water? Aw yes, he said it helped regulate his bowels, but I don't recall our having lemons in the wintertime, back then. Candied lemon *peel*, for cakes, but seems to me like fresh lemons just couldn't be found. Oh, I don't know. Anyway, hot salty water *or* lemon, either one'd make *me* sick as a dog."

She loaded the table with food, poured coffee, and sat down. "How's your head? Don't you want me to—"

"Nope. It's fine." He ate slowly, watching her take her time making a bacon sandwich with a buttered biscuit and peach jam. She ate the sandwich, helped herself to egg. He thought, bemused, that she had not said a word last night and her errand of mercy. Unnatural. Damned peculiar, was what it was. She cast a little glance at him through her sparse eyelashes. Jim relaxed, thinking, "Now."

"That old hinny of Barnes's got over the fence again. Helentaylor hasn't got a rose left, to talk about."

"Um."

"I told her if it was me, I'd just walk right in to the Barnes's yard and cut me some roses whenever I wanted some. I wouldn't ask so much as a *by* your leave."

"Uh huh."

"She's been telling him about that fence for three years. Now, I call that fair warning."

"Sure is."

"The last time it happened he promised to fix it. That was last spring. Late. No, I reckon it was earlier than that. A Saturday morning, I recall. You'd gone in to town, and I walked over—now *why* did I—aw, yes. I'd promised her a setting of eggs. The Rhode Island Reds." Jim felt the morning going, imagined the sun was now in the middle of the sky. "Those Domineckers of hers didn't do anything but eat, seemed like. Well, for Lord's sake, why didn't you tell me the biscuit plate was empty! Me rattling on—you'll be late for work, first thing I know."

"I'm in no hurry." He said it slowly, but she acted as if he had not spoken. She grabbed the plate and ran to the stove, taking a pan of biscuits from the oven, "whewing" and leaning back from the heat. Jim decided that it was early after all, but he might as well take the initiative.

"She tell you about the hinny this morning, or last night when you were over there?"

Effie snatched biscuits from the pan as if they were live coals, too intent upon avoiding injury to reply. He tried again.

"Did you see the damage by lantern light?"

Effie burned her fingers. She shook her hand from the wrist helplessly, darting agonized glances at the butter dish on the table. Jim saw it mysteriously as a distracting maneuver. He would have no part of it. He timed his next remark by the peak of her discomfort.

"Looks to me like you're kind of flustered." She turned all the way around, belligerent.

48

"Now, what about!" Her hand dropped to her side, forgotten.

"Damned if I know."

"Well, I'm not." She brought the bread to the table, poured coffee with the poor burned hand, favoring it not at all. Jim was fascinated.

"Atta girl," he said, enjoying himself for unknown reasons. "Can't get flustered this early." He tried to catch her with some of the unknown. "*Today*, that is."

Her eyes flickered but she refused to bite. She leaned on the table for a moment, then slid into her chair.

"Well, I'm not," she repeated, picked at her egg, then added, "Thinking about that hinny, I reckon. Boils my blood. I wouldn't put up with it." She let her feelings out full on a cloud of discrimination. "Damned old GET of a MISmatch!"

Jim took advantage of her loss of control by stopping eating and plucking at his plate to make her think he had found a hair. If that didn't work, nothing would. When she looked up in alarm he held her eyes.

"Her cousin can keep watch now, can't he."

Effie's face smoothed out, bland as buttermilk, the yellowish drops of sweat like the flecks of butter. She spoke gently.

"It generally happens at night sometime."

Jim was too frustrated to finish his breakfast. He got up from the table, watching her, but she did not remark upon the unfinished food or look at him again. She rose promptly and took the plates to the sink, raking what was on them into the slop bucket. Animosity stood between them like a person. Feeling it, neither one of them would risk revealing it by saying the first, or last, word. Jim took his hat and left.

Effie watched him from the windows, asking herself, "Why? Why?" When he had gone from her view she answered herself.

"Jealous."

"What?"

"Yes. I don't want him to like Jabez. I don't want Jabez to like him."

"*Why?*"

She had herself stumped. She cleaned the house, baked a biscuit pudding, turned on the radio, and sat down beside it to darn socks. Pushing the darning egg into the toe of a sock, something occurred to her. She was remembering the way Jim had tried to lead her by the nose to tell about last night instead of waiting for her to begin in her own way, which had got her back up. After all, it was her story, though he was too proprietary to let anybody else feel they had anything to themselves, a secret or anything. He had treated Will that way. Before Will left he had badgered him about his foreign mail. That was it. Or part of it. One young boy had gone from this place and never come back. Effie blamed Jim. She wondered why.

"Too much flesh."

"Now, *what*—?"

"Too much flesh."

"What does that *mean?*"

"Too much flesh."

She puzzled over it, rocking and darning. She did not generally puzzle herself, she was only puzzled by others. She questioned people avidly, trying to get some clue to the endless fascinations of human nature. Her own nature was simple: she liked order, she feared pain, she would run a mile for a real laugh, and she believed people ought to lift each other up out of the mire. "Throw out the Lifeline" was her favorite hymn. She had stopped churchgoing after she married Jim, because to have gone alone, the only way she could have gone since the unspoken bargain, would have been to make a comment on Jim. She had given up church for him as he had given up drinking for her. It seemed to her that it was a fair enough exchange, for people used church and drink as often as not to hurt others. Lena Barnes, for instance, going every Sunday and sometimes twice just to make a big show of praying for Woody's soul out loud. She was as responsible, in Effie's view, as Woody was, for a nature that allowed him to ignore fences that needed mending. And the hinny, after all, belonged to Lena. Effie thought that Woody was a nicer person than his wife, by which she meant cleaner. Lena washed souls in public but her fat neck was creased with dirt, and she let dishes pile up until they were flyblown. Effie had told her—the reason they were on the outs—"Clean your house or don't expect Jim and me back here." That was after a card game when Effie had almost thrown up at the smell coming from the kitchen. Effie hadn't said it in front of the menfolk and was grateful that it wasn't in her nature to have done so, because Lena, after calling her "Miss High and Mighty" and "Miss Priss," had said, "At least Woody don't have to go to the barn!" and Effie had run off into the night, horrified that she understood, sickened that Lena knew enough to say it.

"How much, oh Lord," she had said then, as now, "of this tribulation is common knowledge?" She had felt betrayed by the world, to the world, a betrayal she had had no hand in, for she had told no one, not even her mama, about the discoveries of her wedding night and subsequently. Would she blame the doctor, to whom they had gone, both of them so embarrassed that they could not look at each other in the office, Jim mumbling, her red as a beet and not able to stop all her tears?

She rolled the socks, put them in Jim's dresser drawer. There the thing was, a harness for a bull, to check its killing nature. Sometimes she handled it, not always without shameful excitement. She remembered one time when she had waited for him, on just such a day after handling the thing, on fire and scared by her body's rebellion against itself. She had given in to her body and gone to the field and dragged him home. Afterward she willfully saw it as a Christian need for punishment, for atonement of some kind through pain. But she knew she could not atone for the hope she had given him, that second year of their marriage, and knowing it—in spite of all she could do—made her despise him. But only at such times.

She sat in her rocker and folded her hands to think. It was important enough to force her idleness. Something was at stake, and if she did not find out exactly what, she would be guilty of worse than idleness when the time came for action.

What Jim was could not be a mystery in the place he had

grown up in. Boys, as well as girls, talked and exposed themselves, evaluated each other, and passed the word along. She could imagine Jim being an object of awe to the other boys, the way a girl with overdeveloped bosoms was to those with titties the size of green peaches.

If she were a young boy exposed to Jim, to *so much flesh*, she wouldn't be able to think of anything else (the way she had envied and hated Rachel Perkins in the eighth grade). It would make her so restless that she would have to get away.

She had startled herself, and then she thought, "Ah yes, Will." The stories about Germany—free love, girls paid to have illegitimate babies. Will had gone to Germany. Jim was responsible.

She protested, then merged with herself. Because of Jabez and her wish to protect him, she tried to sum Jim up as explicitly as she could by gathering together all the bits and pieces of half feelings and thoughts and unmeasurable impressions that she had of him over the years.

"If I were a boy," she said succinctly, "living around him would be like looking at a dirty book, with pictures." Reluctance to dwell upon it halved her again.

"Why?"

"*Because males are excited by the idea of what other males do to females!*" She appreciated the discretion of "male" and "female" as opposed to "man" and "woman." It put the matter in the animal kingdom and allowed her to stay out of it, except as observer. She had observed "males" all her life, watched them watching the mating of brutes, seen the results.

She had watched Jim through a crack in the barn once—just as Lena had; how else had she known?—and though she believed it would be wrong to count what she saw against him, she could not for a second believe that others, including Lena, would feel what she had felt, which was simple gratitude after the first shame and shock. It wasn't even *that* she was really referring to now. Watching Jim milk a cow was somehow worse. What his hands did without knowing; what they did in his sleep.

Last night. She had tried to creep into bed without waking

him, had run into something and froze, had found that it was his hand hovering in the dark waiting for her. She had stood beside the bed while he ran his hand over her belly as though he expected to find it changed.

"My God," she had said, pushing his hand out of the way and lying down. "You scared me out of a year's—" His hand sought her breast and she stiffened and went silent. The fingers kneaded the breast, downward toward the nipple. The palm of the hand did not touch the breast but arched above it as if, in its imagination, it rested on a higher mound. Even asleep, as it turned out he was, he could make her guilty for being so flat-chested.

While his hand worked at her his shattering snores filled the room. She had felt safe then, and removed the hand and arranged herself for sleep. She did so by propping her head high on the pillows and crossing her wrists upon her stomach, palms of hands turned down. Junie, with whom she had shared a room through childhood, always complained that Effie slept like a dead person and that it scared the daylights out of her to wake up and see her sister lying like that.

She had lain thinking with pleasure of young Jabez, who, she had decided, must be a kind of genius. He had played the pump organ for her and sung songs and read to her out of a big book of poetry. He behaved as though they had known each other all their lives. He had even petted her on the cheek! She thought she had read somewhere that true geniuses were delicate, or what ignorant people called "sissy." If they were women, they acted mannish. She considered the idea of taking up smoking.

Something in him had simply drawn her; she had never felt such a pull to anybody. She had begun, even before she left (Helen Taylor came in finally at ten forty-five; she had had to hitchhike on the highway!), to envisage a changed future, made unpredictable and exciting by the boy. He was nervous as a bird, darting around; you never knew where he would light or what he would say. Just thinking that had made Effie yearn in the darkness, discarding like an old shoe her general attitude that comfort came from certainty, and from

53

certainty, order. That really only applied to the chore of daily living and the placement of objects. Alone with herself, she did not mind that she was all contradiction.

It was then that she had become aware that something had been bothering her, a sound as if a wind rustled the window shade, and yet the night was as still as death. She listened carefully; the sound was right beside her ear. Jim's hand was still moving.

Gingerly, in curiosity mixed with guilt, she placed her hand softly over his and followed its movements. It was an unpleasant thing to do, like trying to identify an animal in the dark by the way it dug its hole, but she managed to keep her hand on his and found that his fingers were pulling at a corner of the pillow, which they had twisted into the shape of a nipple.

She wished to slap the hand hard, as she would any dirty boy's. She tried to think about young Jabez again, and even that made her angry. He had told her that the boys called him Bessie. She would like to get her hands on all crude, ignorant boys who caused pain and heartache and wring their jaws for them.

She turned on her face and said into the pillow, "It's not my fault." She tried to summon her mother's face to nod and smile her over the hump of nameless guilt, a hill that often seemed to stand between her and pleasant sleep. As long as it was nameless she could count on her mother to encourage her to dream, so she would not try to name it for fear it was something her mother could not approve of. Effie knew, no matter what Jim thought, that her mother could not be counted on to take Effie's side indiscriminately. She would abandon her daughter to sleeplessness without a qualm, if need be.

"Oh, Jim," she had said fretfully. She had half hoped that he would wake up. At such times she felt that if they could just talk to each other, unseeing in the dark, just eardrums and voices without the rest of the bodies' burden, something might happen, something important that would change their lives, though she never could go one step further and imagine what it might be.

She got up from the rocker and went into the kitchen, to reconnect herself to the day. The sight of Jim distantly in the fields, almost a speck yet not mistakable for anyone else, made her continue. It was also the way he moved that revealed him; the way he ate and spoke and the way he listened to the radio. It was his very nature that she referred to, and his nature was dangerous.

She was as detached as if it were some strange criminal she described instead of her husband. And yet she trusted her feelings. She knew those. But it came to her that there was margin for error in her conclusions. She was a fair person, and shy, and her fairness overrode her shyness in this case as she came to the decision to take Helen Taylor fully into her confidence. She would share with her friend all the facts at hand, including the nature and size of her true cross, and see if they agreed on the matter of too much flesh and Jabez.

Effie met Jim's swelling dark silence at dinner and supper with general comments, framing her solicitude about his lit-erally swelled head in a manner which required no answer. After supper he sat on the front porch for such a long time that, growing sleepy, Effie grew worried, for it was always on those nights when she was first in bed that she had to suffer his passion or whatever it was he felt for her then. Early in their marriage she had discovered that the way to avoid sex with him was to stay up until he was asleep.

Once or twice, in addition to the one day of her curious passion when she had got him from the fields, she had delib-erately gone to bed first. Afterward, trying to remedy the pain with compresses and salves while Jim slept, she would see herself as a crazy woman, or an unchristian martyr headed for hell. Once he had ignored her signal, which she saw was double meanness, and for which, crazy woman, she could not forgive him.

But tonight, with purity distilling in her brain, she was not about to risk fermentation just because she was so sleepy. The one way to handle the situation was really not fair to Jim, the tired farmer enjoying the air on his own front porch, but life itself was not always fair, and who was she, Effie Cummins, to ignore the great example?

She went out and sat beside him in the swing. He promptly got up and went in the house and to bed. He was snoring so soon after that Effie felt excused: he had plainly been dying for bed, but again his pride insisted that she and not sleep should be the force to drive him there.

"Well," she thought, creeping in beside him like a mouse, "you might as well get used to being the crook, Miss Priss. It'll be a change for him, anyway."

The next day was Saturday, and on the evening of that day Effie took Helen Taylor fully into her confidence while the radio broadcast Nashville to the southern half of the United States and young Jabez, after tickling the ladies with a mean imitation of Roy Acuff (he preferred classical music), went out to stargaze and watch for the hinny.

It seemed to Effie that he knew she wanted to be alone with his aunt—he was a nephew and not a cousin, as she had told Jim—without her having to say a word, and the idea that they were so in touch with each other so soon, and his tact, almost took her breath. It added stress to her tale, and the two ladies bent, one on each side of the radio, toward each other, closer and closer.

As Effie approached the crucial part her voice dropped, as though Nashville could hear her through the radio. Helen Taylor, who could not hear her, lowered the volume once, twice, bending ever nearer, until she and Effie were head to head, leaning with ears pressed against the radio for the increasingly distant reassurance of The Grand Ole Opry. The talk stirred them both, and when Effie told of her wedding night, and then of the device that failed, the partial relief made her feel that she would like to go one last step and scream it out, and she stopped herself just in time by realizing that she was only talking about, and was not, after all, experiencing, the real thing, though all the usual feelings and reactions were there in her body; except, of course, the real thing.

Helen Taylor, bosom heaving, eyes glittering in the light from the kerosene lamp, seemed to sense Effie's need to scream and grabbed her hands, holding them in a grip meant to be tight and comforting but that, as the climax approached, became so viselike that Effie thought she might have to go on and scream anyway.

Afterward they had a home-brew apiece and talked theory. Effie timidly presented her belief that men, by their actions and talk, acted upon each other like Spanish fly on a stud animal. She felt more than half a fool and dreaded the possibility of her friend's laughter, especially after her total success earlier. She could have fallen to her knees in thanksgiving when, instead of laughter, she heard Helen Taylor say, in her beautiful, precise voice:

"I cannot but agree with you, at least insofar as men who frequent restaurants are concerned. I have heard them talk—I, and the other girls—as we waited to serve their tables just behind the swinging kitchen door with the pane of glass in it, at their so-called "business luncheons." And others, too. The drinkers—" here she faltered for a moment—"who request the back tables so that they can conceal their *whiskey*—" setting drinkers apart from Effie and herself—"beneath the table cloth. One group of six, and I shall never forget it so long as I might live, came into the restaurant one evening, oh, a year or more ago, and took the back table, and they drank and they talked about where they were going and *what they were going to do*—" She came to a dead halt, changing color.

"Well, go on!" Helen Taylor could make even the most horrible story, or the most boring, marvelous to Effie by the way she used the American language. She had taught school for almost a year once, when she was barely in her twenties, substituting for a regular teacher who had had an appendix removed followed by complications. Her dream of making a career of teaching had not been realized, but the experience had left a permanent mark, and she uttered every word as clearly now as she had then, to her first-grade pupils.

"Go on, dear," said Effie, suffused with a warm glow which she interpreted as love, although her drinking, like her confessions, was rare and marvelous. She was a bit dizzy, but she did not think it was the home-brew that made her appreciate her friend's ability to take her own common, hard-won thoughts and make them sound deep. "*Do* go on, dear Helentaylor."

"—to *one girl*," said Helen Taylor, deciding to brave it out in spite of remembering that the one girl was Effie's sister, Junie. She thought: How much I have to keep from her! remembering Ludie, but Effie's not knowing about Ludie at least made it allowable for her to have young Jay to stay with her. In the silence that gave Effie time for gratifying reaction to what had been told her, Helen Taylor continued her thoughts: How very much I have to protect her from. Perhaps this is the real basis of our friendship, that she needs protecting and I fulfill that need.

She thrilled to the fact that Effie seemed to be actually asking her to side with her against Jim, an opportunity that had never occurred even in her dreams. A practical woman, she dreamed only the possible. But look at the possibilities now! Still, she must move slowly and take a step only when the ground had been tested and proved firm beyond the shadow of an error.

"—the point being," she went on aloud, seeing that Effie was waiting for the moral—or, she could not help thinking, the immoral—"that those young—those six men worked upon each other's feelings like—oh, I don't know what!" She despaired that she totally lacked a gift for comparing one thing with another, pointing out similarities the way even the most uneducated seemed to do with no trouble. She had always dimly felt that that was the reason she had not been allowed to go on teaching. Her friend saved her.

"Exactly!" said Effie. Helen Taylor thought, as she spoke further, that perhaps she should have plied her first-grade pupils and their parents and the school examiners with home-brew, if that was what it took to make her seem brilliant.

"One of the girls," she went on, "said that she had read somewhere that statistics proved most rapes took place after mens' club meetings—smokers, I think the term is. So you see!" She believed that she glowed with successful effort, but thought with an inward giggle that if she were a horse the "glow" would be called sweat.

"Then you do agree about Jabez?" Helen Taylor had forgotten what it was she was supposed to agree with, and at her doubtful expression she saw Effie's face crumple.

"Oh, Helentaylor. We just can't let Jim drive him to rape and death, the way he did Will. We can't!"

"Oh." Helen Taylor's relief was profound. "Honey, I don't think Jay's going to rape anybody. I doubt if he could, he's so small, you know, and I doubt if he'd want to anyway. He's a comfort and blessing, he really is, but—"

She decided not to tell Effie something else: that when she came home from work last night, Jay had met her with his face made up like a chippie's, lipstick, rouge, mascara, and would have got up that way for Effie's visit if his aunt had not reasoned with him. She told him: he knew it made no difference to her; she was not like her brother, and he was as welcome as she didn't know what to her dresses and underthings, too, if he wanted to dress up. But didn't he think it would be best to confine such conduct to the house, which should not—didn't he agree—include the front yard? And to those times when there were only the two of them? His bad experiences at home should let him see the wisdom of this.

Of course, if he had been otherwise, she would not have got him—"For keeps," his father, her brother, had said, among other things, many of which she had had to keep from entering her head by an act of will. Oh, she had heard them but they were gone now, thank heavens. Or would be gone soon, she fervently hoped. Anyway, if he had been otherwise she could not have borne to have him around, not even for a visit. She had neither lover nor husband, had never had either one, and she did not, at the age of fifty-three, want to have around her a constant reminder of those facts, and such a reminder a more masculine boy would have been.

With Jay, she could act as she had with Ludie—both of them her brother's leavings, but she was not proud. She had loved Ludie and would love Jay, no matter what. Last night, dressed and made up, he had reminded her so much of his sister that she had nearly called him by her name. Everything she thought about that haunted girl made her want to march up the road to the Cummins house and fell Jim Cummins with an ax, though she knew pretty well that his jilting Ludie had, at most, only brought on sooner what everybody said would have happened later. It was the terrible blood on her mother's side. The whole family . . . but she could not bear to think about it and how it might affect her future, or her heart would break in her breast and split her from corner to corner. Effie was talking. She must pay attention, *must* keep on the lookout for any and every opportunity—

"—keep on the lookout," Effie was saying so fiercely that Helen Taylor wondered if she had spoken aloud, if the jig was finally up. Then, seeing Effie's sodden expression, hearing her voice screeching on in the room, Helen Taylor thought, feeling pale and mushy inside as a creamed onion—"Why, I do believe she hates her husband as much as I do."

A tapping at the door sent the suspended ladies hurtling toward each other so that their home-brew bottles clinked together as if in a toast.

"Finished?" asked Jabez, peering around the doorframe. The ladies welcomed him, and as he advanced into the room it seemed that he was made of cobwebs. Helen Taylor, who sometimes drank several home-brews at a sitting, and so was more sharp-eyed than Effie, saw that the boy's cheeks were meshed with the fine pattern of screening; window screening. The radio sat on the table exactly in front of the window. The window was screened, sash flung high to the summer night. "And on top of that," his father had told her, whispering or shouting, she could not recall which, "he *listens*." To which she had retorted, "Well, I should hope he does," determined to have him at all costs.

Looking at the evidence on the boy's cheeks, she smiled, thinking, "I have him." She turned her smile to include Effie, and amended her thought: "We have him."

Effie gave her such a clear look, cutting through the drunkenness, it was as though she were saying, "He is our secret. Our son." Both ladies blushed.

By Wednesday night Jim had a secret of his own. He was being followed. On Monday morning, early at the branch, he had felt a presence and craned and peered to no avail, finally concluding that it was an animal, driven by the drought to seek water in the daytime, which lurked in the bushes waiting for him to leave. But when he left, the presence went with him. Not immediately; on the sledge and in the center of fields he did not feel it, but when his work brought him near hedgerows and clumps of trees, it was there waiting for him. Then abruptly it had gone, sometime in the late afternoon.

When it reappeared or was refelt on Tuesday—early, at the branch—he had called out, "Who's there?" If it was an animal, his voice would send it threshing away through the bushes and trees. There was no answering sound, which meant that it was a person. Somebody. Some *body*, he thought nervously. It was a single presence that he felt. How often in the past had he felt a plural presence, and pinpointing the likeliest spot, would rush toward it shouting in mock anger, flushing flights of giggling pickanninies; in those days his pockets had been kept stocked with hard candies, rewards for, as he called them, "the little spy birds."

The sense of the presence had continued intermittently through Tuesday, and on Wednesday Jim saw his pursuer, or was allowed to see him. The boy appeared between two trees that framed a natural doorway into an ivy-hung clump of scrub that had been let stand in the middle of the west field, now shoulder-high with corn; the scrub was ancient and hard as rock, like an above-ground cave. As Jim approached it behind the plow he thought he saw a flicker of color, and it was when he deliberately rested at the end of the row on the field's perimeter, scanning the clump for further evidence, that the boy appeared between the two trees, walking out slowly and returning Jim's gaze for maybe half a minute. Then he had disappeared, or so it seemed to Jim. One second he was there, the next he was not. When Jim once again neared the clump on the opposite side he watched out for the boy, so concentratedly that the plow, untended, roamed into and uprooted some stalks of corn.

Jim was angry and turned his anger against the clump, asking it what in hell it wanted, but there was no answer. He felt absence as he had felt presence. The rest of the afternoon he approached likely hiding places with what he admitted was anticipation, but there, too, he felt only absence. It was not until he was working in the barn, close to sundown, that there was once again the sense of someone near. The effect upon him was like relief.

It had been in his mind to call the boy out and confront him, or try to, when next he was given the chance, but feeling the nearness, he thought that the silence involved a kind of communication that he had never known except with animals, and it was this mysteriousness, the surprise of it, that made him unwilling to risk spoiling it with words.

He asked himself what they could say to each other that would be half as interesting as the silence, which was like a heavy package tied with many knots. The package could hold a bomb, because it was wartime and he had had a Nazi brother, or it could hold nothing. Between the bomb and nothing there were all the possibilities in the world. Between death and nothing was what he found he meant, and the thought made him sweat, the way he had as a kid when he had tried to imagine what *forever* meant, or still did when he looked down his future without the protection of his past. At such times it was as if he hung head down over swift water, grabbing at the fleet unidentifiable shapes below the surface. It was not in his nature, the nature encouraged and permanently scarred by Miss Ethel, to take for granted that shapes glimpsed in water were always fish.

He brought himself back to place and purpose. He was again alone; he knew it beyond doubt. Connecting the two places—Miss Ethel's little book-lined room and the barn—he said aloud a riddle his father had been fond of saying when nature acted up, which applied equally to people: "A farmer knows too much about nature to think he knows anything about nature." He clanged the milk buckets together for emphasis and started toward the tack room. He almost dropped the pails at the sound, very near, of hands clapping.

"Now, what the hell!" He spoke belligerently to the near dark, turning slowly, holding the buckets at $45°$ angles from himself, half expecting one of them to come up against a body and spill the milk. Even as he did so, in real anger, the intrigued part of himself hoped that there would be no answer. There was not.

He finished his chores, not knowing whether or not he was being watched. He had believed that he was equipped with something like a radio aerial which picked up signals and transmitted them to him when another person was near. This part had now been thrown into doubt, and he wondered how wrong he had been in the past, especially as regarded his most personal activity in the barn. He believed that the thought would have to alter his future, and it was like a cold hand closing slowly on his cods, cutting off the seed.

III

Jabez wound the Victrola as tightly as he could without snapping the spring. The urge to give it one more turn was nearly overpowering. He stood for a long time with his hand on the crank, feeling the dangerous tension in his palm. A hair's-breadth beyond the space his knuckles occupied in the air lay the destruction of music. A great twanging noise, or a dull small pop? The possibility of the dull small pop was where the trouble was. For the certainty of the great twang he would have pressed on.

But great things often died small deaths. An immense trumpeting elephant crept away in secrecy and gave up a ghost as small as a baby's. Oscar Wilde, whose falling should have shuddered the earth, drooped and expired with no more racket than a wild flower. Jabez released the handle and heard the Victrola squeak in relief. His frustration was so intense that he cast about for some other victim. He could break the record; he knew all the songs by heart and could play and sing them until the cows came home.

"Until the *cow* comes home," he said with the sweet savagery which his aunt and Effie found so adorable, thinking of his aunt's pendulous bosom. He clasped the record with both hands, pressing his thumbs over the spindle hole.

"And the little bull," he chanted, beginning to be amused. "The itty bitty bull that would like to get on top of Auntie and make milk." He flooded his mind with a picture of his aunt and Effie in violent coitus.

"Cow-tus," he said, delighted, sinking into a chair and pressing the record, perilously tautened, between his spread legs. He thrust himself toward the record, his thumbs making room for his unerected penis to bump against the tiny hole. He went "Ahhhhhh, ah, ah, ah, ah" in imagined parody of Lesbian passion. He was his aunt and the tiny hole was Effie, splayed over the large white expanse of stomach. Then, as Jay-Jabez-Bessie, he moved around and observed the women from all angles.

Effie's skinny legs strained to encompass his aunt's blubbery girth, forcing the cheeks of her behind to spread to where he could see the other hole. It looked as if it had eaten a green persimmon, puckering in distaste. He plunged his finger into the hole and Effie screamed, writhing over his aunt like a frog on a gig, trying to escape.

Jay, the scientist, observed that where the friction was greatest between the two bodies there was a layer of gray powder, like that obtained by rubbing two porous stones together. There was no sweat, no body oil, no lubricity—a favorite word—and at the same time it was the lewdest act he had yet invented for them. He had had them lapping at each other like cats, humping like dogs; he had had them attached at the breasts, a version of the Siamese twins, and he and Jim had pulled them from behind until the mutual dugs had stretched as thin as rubber bands, then released them. The one thing he had not allowed them in his fantasies was penetration by man. He withheld that fulfillment from them as zealously as he would have in real life if he had been able, knowing what he did about the taint women carried in their bodies, the bad blood that could rub off as it had on his father.

He was in exile from all the pleasure and pain of home because his father had succumbed to the infection his mother carried. His father was a dumb, good-looking ass, dumb and doomed, because he had not had the sense to lay off his wife while there was still a chance. He had not had it in his blood, the way his children had at birth, and could have run away. But he was getting crazier by the day, had become a madman the last time Jabez saw him.

Jabez pressed his hands to his face, his fingers kneading his temples. The released record fell to the congoleum and rolled, wobbling, to the hearth and broke against the grate. The sound released Jabez, and also released his desire. Desire pushed at the front of his pants, and as he rose from the chair the seam in back pressed into him like a finger. He walked to the Victrola, tingling with the sensation that someone was behind him touching him, and placed a record on the turntable. He pushed the lever to SLOW and lowered the needle into the groove.

The sung words were hardly more than a growl at the slow speed, coarse-textured and bestial as the utterance of something half dog, half Negro. He unbuttoned his pants, growling the words along with the record. "Myself when young did eagerly frequent," but with the punctuation of harsh, painful breathing and long drawn-out snufflings of the slowest speed, he and the record went: Muoiaseelfff huhwheeaann uooahnnnnng.

Erected, he recalled his vow of celibacy. It had been taken with his hand on one of the two sacred objects he possessed, his copy of the *Rubaiyat* of Omar Khayyam. (The other sacred object was a prism; both it and the book had been stolen from the Memorial Library where he had worked for part of last summer, when he was thirteen.) The *Rubaiyat* was not only sacred because of its truth and beauty. It was also magical and awesome for reasons other than its contents. It was almost as old as the dawn of civilization, having been printed in England in 1859, a mere five years after the birth of Oscar Wilde. There were the magical words and numbers: "First Edition, England, 1859," and above them, in wavery writing like dried brown blood, the inscription: "To My Beloved."

He had stolen that particular copy because there was no signature, no sexual identification to interfere with his imagination. "To Eunice" would have spoiled it, or "Yours, Horace." Even the wonderful name, Saki, which he found in later editions, would have been intrusive, lessening the magic. "To My Beloved" was the world to itself, a hand to its body.

He crammed himself back into his pants and buttoned up, making haste lest a lingering touch might be construed by the god of the Book as breaking his vow.

Sometimes when he touched the book, the down on his arms and legs, the hair of his head and crotch, even the circles of tiny hairs around his nipples would rise and fall as though someone were passing a bolt of lightning up and down his body. It was fear as well as love that he felt at such times, the love and fear of something greater than life, larger than death, more impenetrable than insanity.

He pushed the speed lever on the Victrola until Lawrence Tibbett sang in a normal voice, "I came like water, and like wind I go," the point at which, under other circumstances, he would have increased the speed to FAST and obtained his satisfaction at the same time that Lawrence Tibbett became a tenor.

Rid by fear of desire and his frustration that he had not been able to find Jim anywhere, the livelong day, Jabez, to further placate the god of the Book, thought kind thoughts.

Effie was cute. She really was. Her teeny tiny eyes like toy buttons on a toy dog. No, a toy chicken. She was like a little chicken, scrawny and cute. Her little teeth were like little grains of seed which she had not been able to swallow. Her wee tongue, which rolled up from each side when she laughed, and stuck out, was like a half-swallowed fishing worm.

Jabez bounded across the room and out the door, shouting at the hinny that was not there, the maneuver meant to distract anyone tuned into his thoughts that had gone sour.

It wasn't just what he had heard on the week end that made Effie and him rivals for the same man. They were natural rivals because they were opposites. When he put on women's clothes it was to show them up for what they were, all except Ludie, who had been like nobody else on earth.

At times when he thought about her he felt as helpless as a baby whose tears are misunderstood. He remembered her things, the good-smelling bottles and drops to put in the eyes. Sometimes she would dress him up and put color on his face, laughing or crying, it did not seem to matter which. The dim relative Ludie called Cow Woman, who locked doors on Ludie whenever she went from room to room, sometimes locking him out, would sit in a corner and mutter and shake her head. He remembered a dress with a yellow train, recalled holding the train up and dancing for Ludie, clattering in her big shoes. Her teeth showed; she hugged and kissed him. She told him, "Go out and play now, sweetheart." He began to untie the sash of the dress; the last time his father had whipped him. "No, honey," she said, "go play the way you are." He was scared. Ludie said, her breath on his face, "I'll watch from the window." "That youngun's goin to get whupped," said Cow Woman. Ludie told her, "Mind your business, bitch." She looked at Cow Woman, her mouth twisted at one corner so one cheek looked very fat as though it had eaten the other. Jabez laughed at the funny face. "Go on," Ludie said and gave him a push. Klomp klomp went the big shoes as he hurtled laughing into the locked door. "Open it, Cow," his sister said. Cow Woman's face was purple as she got up and stabbed the door with the key, twisting it so that the lock groaned. "He's goin to whup you." Jabez heard that she was worried for him. From the other side of the door he heard Ludie saying, "If that bastard touches him—" and Jabez felt enclosed by a high wall which his father could never climb. He sat on the top step of the stairs and began to scoot down, the train flowing behind him. Through the glass front door he saw a rocking chair skittering like his billy goat and saw his father give it another kick. On each side of the locked door he and Ludie screamed and screamed together.

Later he watched Ludie's eyes jumping so that his father got scared and backed out of the room. Right after that Ludie had gone away, and he had not seen her again.

Her actions had taught him how to scare his father, how to handle even his bitch mother, the narrow-mouthed woman who boasted of her high instep and temper. "Can't find a shoe that'll fit me without having the vamp stretched, and you know what that does to shoes. It's like my high temper, what it does to a man. Let me tell you, I can wear 'em both out soon enough!" Jabez called her Typhoid Mary because of what she carried and transmitted without getting sick herself.

He wandered among the roses left by the hinny, seeing how they lolled, heavy heads fallen forward, their petals creased and used-looking as ladies' summer handkerchiefs.

He wanted to fill watering cans and sprinkle them until they perked up and stood stiff, but he resisted the urge because he knew that once begun he would not be able to stop his imitation of the rain. He would be fetching and carrying and sprinkling until the well ran dry, because in addition to the roses there was the grass, there were the trees—wrinkled leaves drooping from apparently sapless stems. There were the shrubs and weeds and the road itself going to powder until he could smother looking at it.

Across the fields the heat lay suspended like stairsteps to another world, or like the other world itself breaking through the air in patches. He tried imagining that other world composed of vapors, circling a grassy sun, but saw that the heat had rendered this world as dreamlike as the imagined one, and therefore might it not be the same?

Like Alice, he stepped into a place of opposites where the perverse was the rule and the old rules were violations of this country's order. Effie, stepping down the road like a circus pony, trying, it was plain, by pulling her knees nearly to her chin with each step, to somehow walk on top of the dust, was an object to arouse loathing and threats of the death penalty: *A woman who did it with a man.* Jabez had heard of such things, but to think *there was one in this part of the country.*

"Hoo hoo," she cried, waving. "Am I too early?"

Waving back, Jabez said in a normal tone, "Wherever you are, it's too early," then shouted to her, "For what, Miss Ef?" seeing it like the word on a board fence: Miss F – – –.

She astounded him by tripping forward in little bird steps which, stopping, she seemed to reconsider before she resumed, changing the tiny affected steps into large, for her, and mannish strides. She strode forward, holding out her hand, and when he took it she gave him a brotherly grip surprising in its firmness. It was as though she were trying to match his fantasy of her, for when she spoke her voice attempted a manly gruffness which almost made him laugh in her face.

"For the poetry reading, Ja-*bez*." From her pocket she took a sack of tobacco and some papers. "Want to roll 'em?" she said. He did laugh then, and Effie with him. "Oh, Lord," she told him, sinking into the porch swing, "I don't know what's come over me. I haven't smoked since I was about ten. We used to smoke cornsilk, but once, I think it was just once, we all shared a corncob pipe with real tobacco in it. Some of us got sick. But—" she added with pride—"I didn't. Still—" she eyed his hands rolling with expert quickness—"I don't know."

"Everybody smokes in New York," he told her.

"Well, then—" She handed him a kitchen match, which he lit by rubbing it along his haunch.

"And," he told her, exhaling a pungent cloud, "everybody paints their fingernails, too."

"Men—?"

He nodded, giving her the cigarette and starting to roll another. "Boys, everybody. I read it in *Vogue*. Boys just use the clear, but men go in for Jungle Red."

She laughed, looking inward, then shared with him. "I was trying to see Jim's big paws all painted up." She so plainly regretted having said the name that Jabez did not, as planned, ask where Jim was. Sitting by her side in the porch swing, both of them smoking, Jabez recited "Thanatopsis." From the moment that he gave the title, he saw her mind wander, though now and then her mouth would pinch up as he recited as though expressing disapproval. Without pausing between poems, he gave her also "The Harlot's House," wondering if she would notice the difference in cadence and substance, feeling like a scientist experimenting with a small animal. When he was silent she said, "Neither of those men was a Baptist, I can tell you that."

He was sorry that she was so quick.

"Now you say one, Miss Effie."

She launched with great energy into "Little Boy Blue" but flagged midway, saying, as though angry, "I don't give a damn for those sad stories. They made us learn that one or I wouldn't have. I had a teacher—" She decided against and then for continuing, "Well, she used to cry over that poem something pitiful. Her own baby died."

"Legitimate?"

She tried not to be shocked. "I said she was a *teacher*, Jabez."

"Married or not, they all fuck."

Her jaw fell. She started to rise. Jabez bounded out of the swing, yelling at the hinny that wasn't there for the second time that day. Finding her still glazed when he returned, he squinted his eyes and gritted around his cigarette, "Forget it, kid. I thought you were one of us." His Humphrey Bogart was wasted on her.

"Us?"

"Poets." He expounded, giving the words time to sink in. "We don't care about morals, religion, any of that stuff. We say what we want to, in front of anybody, even preachers. Poo poo on Jesus and all that bunch."

She stared at him, her face becoming slowly animated with tics. When he cautiously shifted out of her reach she broke down. She held herself and rocked back and forth, then got up and staggered down the steps. When she could manage to she said, "If you don't beat all. I swear you'll be the death of me. Right from the minute we met—" She went off again into squawks of laughter, shaking her head, tears on her cheeks.

He jumped down beside her, cavorting to prolong the laughing fit. "*What* when we met?"

"I said to myself, 'That boy's going to free me!' And it looks like you have. I swear I haven't laughed like that in—"

"Free you from *what*, Ef?"

"Now—" She gave him kindly warning at the liberty. He showed quick palms in apology, another movie gesture he admired, and she did not follow up the warning with a lecture, which won his approval.

"Well, Miss Effie, for what?"

She wiped her eyes, teased, "I'm not going to tell you."

"From being a prude?"

She looked astonished, and he saw that he had nearly showed his hand. Soberly she told him, "A farm woman can't afford to be a prude. It's not prudish to—" With perfect judgment, he saw her recalling that he was a boy, just at the moment of telling him something. He knew the look. He watched her narrowly as she ruminated, then asked with cold impatience, "What then, madam?"

Her anger was instant. "Now you just hold on!" When he

showed his innocent bewilderment she cooled off and explained. "My mother wrung my jaws when I called her that. I cried like anything, but all she'd say was it wasn't respectful. I didn't know what she meant until I was full grown."

"Whorehouse," he said, and she nodded. Bored with her stops and starts and prissiness, he told her, "Well, it's French for Mrs., but I guess the stupid bitch didn't know that." She swung at him with open palm, her arm drawn all the way back, but he danced away from her chanting, "Freedom, freedom" until he saw her give up. But she was not amused, and the look in her eyes told him that she suspected he was not on her side after all. He told her, "I call my mother that because she is, but your mother's probably as smart as a whip."

"You call your mother—Jabez, don't you love her?"

"No'om."

"Now, she loves you."

"Hell hath no fury like a mother's love." He saw her face twitch again and took advantage. "I extend my paw to you in friendship and apology." She took his hand.

"All right, Jabez. But you'll take some getting used to. Go slow, boy."

He sat on the porch steps, having worked up a hangdog expression while his back was turned. When she sat beside him he believed that her suspicion had retreated, though how far he could not gauge. It was with a sense of genuine daring that he tentatively launched his prepared attack.

"I can free you, Miss Effie, if you'll let me." She gave him a look. He could see her rating his sincerity, and when she nodded he went on. "Aunt Helen's garden is little, and scraggly, 'cause the soil there is poor. A rock garden, that's what it grows. Next year—" and he nodded toward the back of the orchard.

Effie approved both his concern and his wisdom. She had always said that the loam back there would produce Texas-size vegetables, for it was the site of a cow barn torn down some years before. But Helen Taylor thought a garden, and she always emphasized *kitchen* garden, should be close to the kitchen, where a body didn't have to trudge a quarter mile if she wanted a bunch of parsley. "Why," she said, "a nigra could attack me back there behind those trees and nobody the wiser. Me helpless as I don't know what in the arms of a big buck, my despairing screams all unavailing. And once that happens to you," she said mysteriously, "all you want to do is go back there and just wait." "What for?" Effie asked, but Helen Taylor didn't answer. Effie had the image of her friend waiting in the field with a shotgun as night came on and decided to let the matter rest, but she had been further mystified when her friend said, "I know one such case. Couldn't rest ever after. Ran out the door after every one she saw passing, old or young, single or married." "Wanted to kill 'em all, I reckon," Effie said, not liking Helen Taylor's expression. "Or something—" This had been said with a smirk that was not like any expression Effie had seen on her face.

"—would free you for housework or just resting," Jabez was saying, "and you need your rest, Miss Effie, especially in this weather." Effie nodded, trying to look intelligent. She noted from a long distance that he had the look of somebody holding in a secret. At her nod he jumped up.

"Then I CAN?" His expression then was so akin to the remembered one on Helen Taylor's face that Effie was unpleasantly jolted.

"Can what?" she asked, feeling her heart strangely squeezed.

"You NODDED. You just DID. You said I COULD." Effie asked herself if that could really be foam on the boy's lips. She figured it was because it went with the rolling eyes, pupils rolled entirely out of sight and held that way, once he had got her attention. She wanted to get up and shake him but gentled him, frightened as she was, as she would have a horse.

"Jabez," she said quietly, "sit down, son. My mind went wandering, 'sall. I didn't hear what you wanted. 'Course you can have it, whatever it is, I reckon. Now come on and tell me." Watching his hand slowly unclench she wondered if his affliction was epilepsy, and gagged. She had heard that the tongue could be swallowed, had to be pierced with a safety pin and attached to the collar. But he came so quickly to, in spite of his dragging step as he came toward her, that she chose to believe it was a temper tantrum, just kid show. Junie had been good at that when she was a little girl.

She told herself that it was a combination of the heat and his condition, whatever it was that Helen Taylor had not told the nature of, that caused him to have the tantrum. She had lost her temper, too, and would have slapped him down if she had got her hands on him. She felt herself gasping like a fish out of water. If it did not rain soon they would all go crazy. In her mind there flashed a scene as clear as the picture show, of them all at Junie's wedding, all going crazy. When their mother clawed at Junie's husband's clothes, Effie shook herself like a dog, trying to shake loose at the same time the words she heard—*they all fuck*.

She gave, or tried to give, her full attention to Jabez. He had begun while her mind was at the wedding, and she had missed something, but this time she got what it was she may have promised in her stupid hurry. Her garden was to be taken over lock, stock, and barrel by Jabez. He was to be working around the place all day. He and Jim would meet, would eat together, go off someday together. Or Jabez would go alone, the way Will did. He would be lost, lost to her before she ever had him, worse than "Little Boy Blue." If she still wanted him. He had scared her out of a year's growth. She could step on Helen Taylor for not giving her some warning of how the boy could be. God help all parents. She felt that she had the upper hand, though, and was glad.

"I thank you," she told him, "for considering my health and all. But I am in A-1 condition. Even in this weather," and though the mimicry was slight he heard her and gave her a sly look.

"O.K., Miss Effie. You tend the garden, and I'll do the housework."

"Moving in, are you, bag and baggage, come hell or high water?" She felt that she had been overly sharp until he shook his head and said in a low, totally insincere voice, "I'm not even trying to." She started to tell him, Well, you'd better try harder, because the tone was like a giggle. She said, still sharp, "Well, what *are* you doing?"

"Just fighting, I guess."

"What for, Jabez?"

"Life?"

"Seems to me like you've got plenty of that, and the devil, too." But a doubt was in her mind, and she did not speak as forcefully as she should. She saw again the foamy mouth and walled-up eyes, the clinched hand and dragging footsteps. Her stomach knotted.

"Why?" she said. "Why do you want my garden?" It was a pretty as well as a rich garden, bright, still, with flowers. If it happened that she got mortally sick she would want to be as much as possible in just such a place.

"Why don't you want me there?" His voice was so pinched that she knew he was trying to keep something back, was sparing her some knowledge. A hurt creature, off licking itself, would sound that way if it could talk.

"Why, my Lord, I'm not trying to keep you—" She stopped. She was lying. She had forgotten how much she wanted to keep him and Jim apart. But right now, against the darkness of her suspicions, Jim and everything he was and had was like the soul of life. Those thoughts belonged to the time when she had thought Jabez was innocent. That belief had been disproved beyond any return. And yet, if you knew you were going to die young, would you try to hold onto your innocence?

Jabez brought her to. "Miss Effie, I think there's a reason you don't want me around your place." She was shocked at his mind reading. He made her superstitious like the Gypsies who showed up at the back door in fall weather and tried to tell her things. They wanted her garden, too, but in a different way. Sly and bold-eyed, holding nothing sacred—

"If there was a reason, you'd say poo poo on it, too, wouldn't you?"

"Yes'm, I guess so."

"Why?"

"I'm fighting, I said." He was sullen. Feeling the beginnings of fatalism, she repeated her earlier question.

"Why do you want my garden?"

He drew a circle with his toe, shot her a look that terrified her, and said, "It's not just that."

"*What*, then?"

She watched him take a deep breath. "Because—" He eyed her. She wondered what he was pulling out of her mind. "Because I'm dying."

Having heard it, she squeezed her eyes shut, mourning striking her like tiny fists. Hearing a choked sound, she knew that he was crying and knew that in one more minute she would be bawling along with him, the two of them clutching each other. There was another choking sound followed by a snort. Her eyes flew open. His face was split apart, the way a baby always cried, holding nothing in.

"Of BOREDOM," he yelled, and she heard the words and laughter with disbelief. Instantly she was torn between wanting to wring his jaws for him until her hand hurt, and giving in to the flood of thanksgiving: HE IS NOT DYING.

He had played her like a fiddle. In the course of the afternoon—and how far it had gone on its course she could not guess, only that it seemed like a lifetime—he had got her to recite a poem she detested, accept dirty talk, take lying down his calling her mother a stupid bitch, led her—it had to be his doing—to a picture of her own mother behaving like an old chippie at the wedding, and put her through feelings as sharp and unpleasant as the taste of tobacco in her throat; a taste like the smell of Jim's dirty socks. She wished to punish him.

When he had settled down a little she let him have it. "I don't know—" she said with just the right pinch of deceitful uncertainty to fix his wagon. He got still. "I don't know." She altered it as though it now were settled against him.

"That I'm bored?" His voice was flat and hard as a man's twice his age.

"That that's any reason to turn my garden over to you."

"But," he said, too calm for her taste, "I was offering, Miss Effie, and you sound like I was taking something."

She admitted his point. No matter how you looked at it, somebody to work the garden would be taking a big load off her back. When the work was done right the garden was as hard as any chore she had.

"I'm just a kid." He said it straightforwardly, and she paid her respects to that, wholesome in the cockeyed afternoon. "I know I'm not average. Kids my age don't know half what I know, don't do what I've done, don't want what I want." She probed him with her eyes. "But I'm still just a kid, not even fifteen yet. And I've been kicked out of my home. And I'm by myself the livelong day, with just that little patch of nigger garden to scratch around in." He told her simply, "I could go crazy."

If she asked him, "Are you being fair?" would he ask what she meant or would he know? She looked closely and saw tears in his eyes before he turned away. A person couldn't fake tears, or if they could, they would not try to hide them from you. But what impressed her most was that he had not reminded her that she had actually promised something, and she had. "Of course you can have it," her voice echoed in her mind, and the "I reckon" did not change it. It was honorable of him. As for her, she knew that a promise, however it was gotten, was a thing rigidly kept, if you were a Christian, even if you didn't go to church. God kept His promises, down to sacrificing his only begotten Son.

Her head hurt from trying to sort thoughts into piles. She knew one thing for certain, and that was enough for her: the boy was lonesome, as lonesome as herself.

She got up, brushed at her seat, and said, "It's yours." He turned, not understanding. "My garden's yours. It's your garden. Let me have a few days to—" and though she stopped, she saw, or thought she saw, that he knew what she had started to say. If so he was on her side, and that was a beginning.

They shook hands, and Effie left. She walked up the lonesome dusty road thinking that she had dipped, for the first time today, into the world. She thought it was as dusty as this road. A funny thought to have about an afternoon with a fourteen-year-old boy, but she was sure he could teach her how the world was, just as she was sure that most of what he

77

taught her she would not be glad to learn. He had made her revise her thoughts about him, and she was saddened and felt like a clown to have been so wrong. The friendly joy she had felt going to him down this same road was not with her when she returned.

"She's not dumb enough," Jabez told the spiders in the cellar as he sacrificed their homes to his haste. He took the bottle of home-brew up to the kitchen and opened it. "I told her," he continued to any and all eavesdroppers, " 'It's not just that' about her garden. She looked like she knew what I meant."

Leaning the bottle neck into the corner of his mouth, his tongue flicking into it, he said one of the sacred verses he could not have exposed to her, not for a million dollars, at their poetry reading:

> Then to this earthen bowl did I adjourn
> My lip, the secret Well of life to learn
> And lip to lip it murmured, "While you live
> Drink!—for once dead, you never shall return."

"That man was no Baptist," he said.

Effie showed Jim the second letter from her mother in two weeks. Her pride made her cackle. He could see the two letters nestling together in a bureau drawer in the future, like two eggs discoloring with age. He did not need her to tell him the contents; the wedding, of course, and something in her round-eyed effort to build up suspense informed him that the wedding was to take place sooner than had been anticipated. Therefore it was with malice that he asked, "Is she in trouble?" He watched with satisfaction that he felt to be feminine as Effie turned the question over in her mind, for he could have been referring to her mother. Suspicion of his real meaning lurked around the edges of her reply, like, Jim thought, Jabez in the hedgerows.

"Weeeell, yes. So much work and all." He had been right. The wedding was set to take place in three weeks' time rather than on August 7th, Junie's birthday. Feeling the lure of sharpened senses, he anticipated the part most difficult for Effie to get out, and for him to accept, he had to admit: that Effie's presence at the old homestead was urgently requested. He knew that if the letter were read, the request would emerge in its true colors as a demand.

Effie wanted to go, that much was clear. But—"What about my garden, Je-im?" hands fluttering helplessly, eyebrows working furiously as though at a solution. Which, he saw, she had already worked out. It came too patly from Effie's prim mouth, complete with the too quick denial at the ridiculous notion. "D'ye suppose Jabez—but naw. He's too . . ."

"Delicate?" Jim asked prissily, then let his anger and frustration out on such a gust of released energy that Effie's hands flew behind her to the apron strings. "What in the all fired hell's the matter with that boy, woman? I want an answer, and I want it straight. You've jacked this thing up until it's like . . . I don't know what the hell it's like. Why can't that goddamned boy take care of a woman's garden?"

He saw then that she had landed him; had fished for him, snagged him, and reeled him in like a county champion. He saw himself with distended gills gasping on the shore, entirely at her mercy.

She took advantage thoughtfully, without a yelp or crow. "No reason," she said finally, "that he can't do as well as me. And—" her pause told him how badly he had been hurt. "I don't think you'd have to offer him much, nothing for him to spend money on." Her vagueness did not hide her previous calculations, probably with Helen Taylor's connivance. "A few dollars a week and pickin rights. They don't eat a lot." Defiantly she told him, "You know that little patch of Helentaylor's couldn't keep a couple of cats alive." He had some idea of how much of their garden already went to the tenant house. Seeing his face she forestalled his words: "The boy can be paid out of my egg money."

"Can he cook?" he said brutally, knowing Effie had not taken that hurdle in her trial run.

"Oh, Jim. You can batch." She was weary and to his surprise he felt sorry for her. In a flash he saw the next three weeks, saw her hands flying at her mother's direction, sewing, cooking, cleaning, heard her voice "yesing" everybody with never a show of temper. His woman, solid and tireless as a settler. Why, she could hew the wood and build the house, if need be, for Junie and her old man to screw in, for Junie to be bored in, for her old man to be deceived in soon enough.

"Sure I can," he said, starting for the door, and felt their pride in each other in the space between them like the Holy Ghost descended, wings, or whatever the hell It had, spread in blessing. He paused.

"Going soon, I reckon."

"T'marrah—" At the slight question he nodded without turning.

"Reckon Pone can take you on the milk truck."

"S'what I thought. Won't need much in the way of baggage. Won't be any trouble for him."

"Company for old Pone, good-looking woman like you." He threw her a look, saw her rosy with pleasure, saw that his jest was based in reality: she was as pretty right then as a little old bird, and on the way to the barn he wondered if he could have made himself a pretty wife out of a steady application of such harmlessly flattering words. He saw the possibilities of such words as beeswax hand-rubbed into furniture.

The thought stayed with him, and over supper he rubbed her to a satiny luster, observed with awe the sparkle in her eyes and the fact that her thin mouth grew lips, as though his words drew blood to those surfaces; as though he sucked and nibbled there—which, to his bemusement, he found that he wanted to do. In all their marriage, their kisses had been antiseptic; his tongue had never penetrated, nor tried to, the juiceless hollow behind her teeth. Once he had said to himself, astonished, that Effie did not even spit, whereas Ludie's mouth had always glistened like some bursting rosy fruit. She had chewed Juicy Fruit gum, and the corners of her mouth had collected and retained the runoff. To kiss her had been to drink at the same time.

"Leave the dishes," he said, and saw with grief that he had mistaken all the signs.

"Jim, it's not even dark!" He looked for the pretty wife he had made for himself out of words and attention, but before his eyes she was fading, deflating. She was like a May fly which another doubtless cold woman had taught him the Greek name for: ephemeron, with a lifespan of just one day. Effie had lived a shorter time. She was trying to desex herself. He knew that under her dress her legs, like two panicked old sisters, were pressing together for comfort.

In the kitchen the husk of Jim Cummins sloughed off and left standing revealed the victimized brute, without desire or thoughts of desire. All that was left was the instinct to rut, and if need be to fulfill it, to kill.

He gutted her on the kitchen floor, tore at her with his tusk that required blood for satiety. But she was dry there, too. Husk was all she was, and if she should slough it, there would be no beast and no woman left in its place. There would be nothing.

"Stay," he told her silently, "stay at your Mama's. I'll take my hell solitary." Without coming, or feeling any of the other satisfactions of the rapist, he left Effie crying on the floor. He was too disgusted to go to the barn and whack off, and he walked under a moon as powdery as a woman's compact.

In his moonlit journey up lanes so heavy with dew that he saw it as mockery, he asked the night: "What can I make for myself that's not like you?" and supposed he meant the deceptiveness. You could not change nature by haranguing it, or flattering it; maybe you could not change it at all. The worst part was, there was no balance, no equity, where nature and words were concerned: for every question there was not an answer. Therefore, every problem did not have a solution. He had been all questions and problems, at least since his marriage, and probably before that. Finally, tonight, he saw and accepted his place in the world.

One place that was his was his own bed. He would not sleep with the beasts in the barn. He lay in his own bed, beside the husk he had married, a husk without the mystery of kernels which could hold sustaining milk, or, dried, be parched and give a different pleasure, or be popped open on a fire and buttered and devoured by lovers. What could you do with a husk? Poor folks made dolls out of them for their children. Effie's mother was not poor, but between her and his own mother they had fashioned a husk-doll and married it off to him.

"Poor old girl," he said, and touched Effie and felt her tremble. He took asylum in sleep, his snores continuing to question the night as Effie counted the hours on the bonging clock and imagined herself already safe at home. "This time tomorrow—" she whispered, and was ferociously glad that her father was dead and gone. There would be no men in that household.

She planned to tell Helen Taylor every word and occurrence, waiting for the milk truck, and realized to her humiliated anger, rehearsing the tale in her head, that what she was feeling was sexual excitement. She turned her head toward Jim, trying to see him in the dark, wondering if he could have explained to her why this was so. She would have liked to wake him and ask him while they were both hurt. Victims of accidents talked to each other, telling each other where the pain was. But with her usual stealth she touched him in a safe place and murmured, "Poor old boy."

IV

Jim did not see Effie off on the milk truck, which would have meant a meeting with Helen Taylor.

When he woke up to the dark morning and smelled meat frying he saw that Effie had worked the problem out, and was grateful to her. She would feed him before he went to the barn, the last meal she would cook for him in three weeks. He thought it must be about four-thirty, but before he could check the clock, Effie, hearing him stirring, came into the room and told him a storm was brewing. She was subdued, as though her words might cause the clouds to disperse. The fact of impending rain wiped out all other considerations, and once or twice, moving around in the rooms, they bumped into each other and smiled. When they sat at breakfast a preliminary gust of wind slammed a door somewhere, and Effie bent over her plate shivering, and he saw that it was with pleasure.

"I can't help it," she said, "it's as exciting as the wedding." He nodded, grinning, thinking of all the people just getting up and smelling the rain, breathing, for the first time in over two months, air that did not pain their throats.

"You be scared in the truck? It's liable to be a heller."

"God, no. I'd be willing to swim home." The remark had an edge but he could not hold it against her.

"See you now, water shooting out of your nose."

"Beats dust."

"I'll say." A funny thought struck him. "You be wearing a hat?"

"With a bunch of cherries." They held in their laughter, both of them seeing the hat—the kind horses wore, as Effie said when she bought it—bobbing on muddy water.

"I'll row out and look for it, case you don't come back."

"Three weeks, Jim. 'Sall." He nodded. "Rains that much, you'll have to row out looking for a farm."

"You? What'll you be looking for?"

"I won't be looking."

"What the hell's that mean?"

"Got what I want, 'sall." Yeah, he thought, mama and home. Effie was going *home*, leaving this place and going *home*. When she mentioned this place, if she ever did, what would she call it? Rain jumped on the tin roof of the kitchen, scurried across it, and jumped off into the mulberry tree rattling the dry leaves. The room grew suddenly light, and Effie started slowly out of her seat crying softly, "Oh my God, is that the sun?" Getting up he said heavily, "Source of life," and she said, with such bitterness that they did not look at each other, "Too goddamned much of anything's a source of *nothing*." He ducked his head, agreeing with her, said, "The enemy," and they parted.

When he stood outside it was under the light of a feeble sun, but as he watched, weather flung across the sky as suddenly as though it were a bolt of dark dress goods in the hands of a salesman, and a high wind rose keening and did not lessen. Down the wagon road he saw two figures hurrying, but before he stooped through the low side door of the barn he looked again and saw only one.

Among the restless cattle he listened to the scream of the wind and thought it was like a woman in childbirth, screaming to tear the rain out of the clouds. "This is serious," he said, and turned to go back and tell Effie to stay where she was. But thought, Pone won't take any chances, will pull in somewhere and stay out the storm if it comes to that.

The drumming in the pail of milk from the second heifer was augmented by the thrum of rain on the roof. By the time he got the milk cans to the mailbox and was halfway back to the barn he was blinded by the downpour. It was as heavy as a waterfall he had stood under in the Cumberlands on his honeymoon.

He stayed in the barn at his chores, and in no time at all,

or so it seemed, he could hear the rush of a river down the wagon road, which was cut low and served to carry runoff from his fields. He would not think about his battered crops but would take everything as it came, in its own time.

He went into the shed and found Jabez sitting high in the seat of a haymaker smoking.

"Don't smoke in the barn," Jim said, and the boy climbed down and put the cigarette out carefully on the earthen floor over which water was streaming. Observing him, Jim saw that he did not seem to be pointing out the safety of wetness to excuse his smoking. He chose the driest part of the uneven floor, and when he had ground the butt out he field-stripped it and scattered the remains until no crumb could have been found. Jim took the old piece of singletree with the good hardware he had come for and started out. "Reckon you're out of a job for a spell. No pay for rainy days. Farmer's life."

"Pay?"

"My wife got me to put you on wages, didn't she tell you?"

"Miss F – – –" the boy said. His look and the pause made Jim see what he was aiming at. He suppressed a laugh, thinking the boy was just a low-minded kid, probably regular as anybody else except for his—

"Listen," he said, "my wife—Miss F – – –" and he paused and grinned, seeing the boy's look prove him right about the smutty intentions. "—she's been hinting 'round something silly about you being sick." He picked up the broadest country dialect, the chummy speech used by good ole boys together. "Now you workin for me, reckin I'd better find out. Just whut the *hail's* the matter with you anyways?"

"Deprivation," the boy said, "I ain't had none in a bluuue mooon." His expression was comical. Jim said, "Why, you peckerwood, you. You ain't big enough to fuck a duck."

"Know how to kiss one's ass, though," and he illustrated by pretending to blow feathers out of the way, followed by a quick kiss. The joke was new to Jim, and he laughed heartily, thinking 'There's nothing wrong with him. He's a regular barrel of monkeys.'

"Come on and hep' me, boy," he said, "and earn your wages."

By nightfall the barn was as neat as Effie's house. Jim and Jabez agreed that you could give a party in the tackroom and eat off the floor. The rain had not let up for an instant, and they had worked soaked from dinnertime on, when they had gone to the house to see what Effie had left them to eat at noon. They agreed that if the rain kept up, they would take the automobile and drive over to Salvation for a store supper. Jim said recklessly that he could justify using the gas if he bought a ball of twine from old Huffines. Jabez said he had rather have a Dr. Pepper than all the milk in the world, and a hunk of ratcheese and some soda crackers tasted better to him than chicken pot pie and coconut cake. *Cold* chicken pot pie was what he said, and though it seemed to cast aspersion on Effie, Jim thought that he didn't mean it that way, and agreed that sometimes he felt the same. He said if you threw in some weenies and a dozen or so hamburgers, those little flat gummy kind, he would settle.

"And potato chips," Jabez said.

"Pretzels."

"Clark Bars."

"Vienna sausages."

"Baloney?"

"American cheese!"

"Chili!"

"Bar-B-Que!"

"Pussy!"

"Boy, don't brang that up, my mouth's awaterin already."

"Mine, too," Jabez said, forcing the spit to run from his mouth and dribble down his chin.

"Quit it, feller, you're spoilin my appetite."

Jabez came around the table and put his face close to Jim's. "Kiss me big boy, and take out cha thang."

Jim got up and cuffed him and got in return a blow to the belly that knocked his wind out. "Shit," he said when he could, "you don't hit a man on a full belly." He eyed the boy. "You play for keeps, don't you."

86

"Damned right I do. I'm a tough sumbitch, schweet-hot."

Jim dived for him and pinned him to the floor, pleased to discover that it was not as easy as he would have thought. The boy was not strong, you could feel strings in his arms instead of muscles, but he was slippery and wily and he aimed to win. Pretending to settle comfortably atop him for the duration, Jim asked, "Calf rope, peckerwood?"

"For now, chump, but I'll get mine," and Jabez slanted such a look that Jim was left for a second time without his wind. Christ Almighty, he looked like Ludie. Feeling the body under his was all at once disturbing in two ways: it felt wrong, and it felt right.

He got up, trying not to seem too abrupt, and saw that he and the boy had left on Effie's carpet a place that, because of their wetness, looked like a wallow where beasts had coupled.

"Good thing she's gone a while," Jim said, "she'd have a conniption fit."

Jabez looked at the wallow, smiling slightly. "In three weeks' time it could be worse."

The words made Jim uncomfortable. On the way back to the barn, the boy dashing ahead to get clear of the rain, Jim speculated about any possible relationship, through Helen Taylor, between Jabez and Ludie. He knew he could not ask the boy, and one of the reasons was that he did not want to know. He figured that Jabez could have been no more than five when Ludie was put away, so there could not be much memory of her even if he had seen her.

In the course of the afternoon, the boy working alongside him without complaint or evidence of tiredness, Jim managed to put the matter away from him. Their work was highlighted by more tomfoolery, but Jim steered clear of any challenge to touch as long as he was uncomfortable. He told himself that he would soon get used to the occasional heart-catching likeness the boy had to Ludie, so that touching him would not make Jim feel helpless, among other responses.

Out of a companionable silence, Jim said, "Listen, feller, why'd you foller me around like you done, spyin on me from out the bushes?"

"Wonderin."

"Wonderin *whut?*"

"Where you'd fit." Another slanted look, which Jim ignored, refusing it a place.

"Now, you'd better be plainer than that, ole hoss."

"Is it time?"

That made Jim mad. "Goddamit, time for what?"

Jabez rested the harness he was mending on his knees. "O.K. feller," he said, poking fun openly, then said in an insolent voice, "my interest in people is confined to above the eyes and below the belt."

Jim, on guard, challenged him. "You heard somebody say that."

Jabez shrugged. "Maybe. It's true, though."

"Hell, I reckon that's true of everybody when you consider it."

"No," Jabez said, "some people are titmouses. Mice."

Jim snorted contemptuously, forcing a return to the ironical country boy game, which he felt, without examining it, was a safety measure.

"And you ain't?" he said, as though such a varmint did not exist.

"Wouldn't touch one."

"By Jesus, you ain't been weaned long enough to talk like that. Your mouth's still puckered up from suckin."

"I never did that."

"Your mammy fed you on a bottle? Shit, that ain't even friendly. No wonder you're a curious kind of feller." Jim expected another of the boy's odd looks but saw that Jabez seemed far away and lonely. Gruffly Jim told him, "I was having a joke."

Jabez gave him the look then, compounded by downright meanness.

"Miss Effie told Aunt Helen that you've got the biggest thing in the world."

Jim was conscious of dividing into two sensibilities which with split-second timing debated within him. A lightning decision was made: *you go.* With hardly a visible pause, he began to roll. Barreling like a hoop and whooping, he wheeled around the barn, holding his stomach. The winner thought: He's like all the kids I grew up with, boys and girls, too, just curious about the superman.

Dredging up words from a past that seemed happy he said, "It's big, all right, and I can whup you with it. If it'uz stiff, it'ud break yo' laig."

"We'll see." Jabez took the mended harness into the tackroom, and Jim followed. It was then they spoke with self-congratulation about the results of their labors.

"Reckon we'd better drive by and leave your aunt a note?"

Jabez was clean and slightly comical in a pair of overalls belonging to Effie and one of her gingham shirts. His hair, too long in Jim's estimation, was slicked back. The effect was like a boy from another time, Tom Sawyer or Huck Finn, though Huck had never been so clean except when the Widder had him in her clutches. The thought of giving him Will's old clothes had come up like a weed and been yanked out before it could do any harm.

"Naw," Jabez said, "I told her I'd probably be staying over." Jim did not bother to examine the lift to his spirits. They drove the five miles to Salvation, the only automobile on the road, in water so deep that the Packard felt like a boat. Jim told Jabez that his mother had wanted a good car, and in 1936 had got herself one, saying it would last her lifetime. Jim figured it would last his too, and one of his pleasures was to keep it in perfect condition. Jabez took its beauty and comfort personally, like a compliment to himself, Jim saw, amused, and it pleased him that the boy knew something about what lay under the hood. Observing one moment at a time, Jim thought that their sense of mutual ease grew with every mile.

When they pulled up to the store, driving in under the overhang on the side, Jim paid for his mindless preoccupation with only the present. He saw Jabez as Ludie in the yellow light. How many times had they parked here, rainy weather or moonlit, and honked the horn, which old Huffines hated, for car service. But he would shuffle out with the Coca-Colas, knowing that they knew he would have crawled rather than forfeit the dime. Jabez's head was thrown back, his eyes closed, the shadow of his eyelashes making them seem as long as Ludie's.

Jim gritted his teeth, feeling his eyes sting, and hit Jabez on the leg. The boy's puzzled face told him how hard the blow had been. Working hard to find the old vein and pump present life into it, Jim said, "Come on, youngun, we done got to the trough. Let's eat now and puke later."

It was not until Jabez stuffed enough to earn his disbelief that Jim felt he had returned to normal. When Jabez nibbled instead of crammed, Jim took a mean pleasure in egging him on. "Just one more Clark Bar, boy; have a bite more cheese, feller; how 'bout a grape Nehi this time?" while old Huffines fetched and carried and took his money and finally loosened up enough to say admiringly, "Sure can eat," in his fat man's high squeezed voice. He pretended to like it when Jim told him, "Kid said he wanted to git like you, Mr. Horace. So I told him, 'Eat like a pig, then.'"

Huffines got back at him as they were leaving. Standing in the doorway he said, "Don't you thow up, boy. Ain't got no refugee womern to eat it." He gave a whinny. "Reckon you're a real Christian, Jim, to feed and clothe the needy. Them's Miss Effie's duds, ain't they."

In spite of Huffines' warning, halfway home Jim had to stop the car while Jabez got out and gave his supper to the night, but he was not embarrassed and made no apology. He showed what he had been thinking about as they pulled into the yard. "That man was egnimatical." He slapped his leg and corrected himself, "Enigmatical. Enig, enig, enig, enig." He sounded to Jim like the little motor in his shed which sharpened his tools, to which he fed quantities of fuel until it belched and spilled oil down its sides. He was amused and touched to think of himself having to wipe the boy's mouth with a rag kept for that purpose.

"Pay no attention to Huffines," he said briefly. "There's nothing you can learn from him worth knowing."

In the house he found a clean rag for Jabez to use in place

90

of a toothbrush, telling him to dip it into the saucer of baking soda and salt. He was again amused by this fulfillment of the thought he had in the car but hid his smile.

They went to sleep, Jabez first, in the big bed while the west wind drove the rain like hail against the windows and caused it to tapdance on the wooden floor of the porch. Jim had to get a blanket down from upstairs, the boy was shivering so. After Jabez was asleep, Jim, feeling coolness emanating from him instead of warmth, slid over and gently curved his body to the shape of the skinny, unmistakably boyish back. He rested his hand for a moment on the flat flannel-clad hip. His hand could never mistake that plane for one of Ludie's in his sleep. Securely he let his hand drop over and lie on the bed in front of the boy's belly, encompassing him in warmth. When he fell asleep it was as though he entered it from a dream reluctantly abandoned.

The morning broke on a gray drizzle. Jim dressed hurriedly and quietly and went first to inspect his fields. There was little damage; the tobacco stood up with crisp vigor, and only a portion of the corn had been partially uprooted by the sweep of water which had left small gulleys between the rows. He was filled with thankfulness for his high, rich land and was in a fine spanking humor when he returned to the house. The smell of coffee met him at the back door.

"What's this!" He slapped Jabez on the buttocks as he stood sturdy in his sleepiness by the stove, a slab of bacon laid out for slicing and a knife poised. Trying not to smile, he saw that Jabez had also set out the biscuit board and sifter.

"Where's the flour?" Jabez yawned, Jim pointed.

"That all you put in biscuits?"

Jabez scowled. "I know how to make the goddamn things."

"Well, wash your hands before you mix up my batch." Jim pretended to dodge a punch on his way to the porch and the milk pails. Going to the barn he whistled. Hearing himself, he stopped, but only for a second. His thought that it was somehow unfair to Effie for him to be so chipper without her struck him as foolishness. She was probably clucking like a hen, safe at home with mama. As for himself, not only had his crops weathered the storm, but last night he had the only dreamless sleep he could think of since time out of mind.

"Why," asked Jim, pushing his chair back from the table, "are you so good to me?"

"Can I smoke?"

"First time anybody ever asked me that. Now let me ask you one: could I stop you?"

"Yes."

"Well, you've stumped me." He pondered. "Can a tobacco farmer say 'no' with a clear conscience to a feller that wants a butt after breakfast? 'Specially when the feller's cooked it? And damned good, too. I reckon that'd keep me awake nights, Jaybird."

Jabez pulled the string on the tobacco sack closed with his teeth, his other hand rolling a neat tube. Through his teeth he asked, "Could anything keep you awake, Jim?"

"Why'd you ask?"

"You slept through a hell of a storm last night, thunder, and lightning." Jabez tucked the sack in his shirt pocket, licked the cigarette, and lit it. "I watched you. Your eyelids didn't flicker. You never stopped snoring." He blew a big smoke ring and a smaller one through it.

"I'm a good sleeper, Jay. Clear conscience. For instance, I never stop a feller from smokin."

"It was like daylight. You kicked the covers off. I put them back on you." He grinned to himself. "After a while."

"Whatever that means," Jim said, knowing what it meant. "Well, I thank you," he said formally, covering his displeasure at the sneakiness.

They washed the dishes together, and Jim told Jabez to stay in the house and wait for his aunt, and then when she was gone to come on to the barn. But when he heard Helen Taylor approaching the barn, singing out her warning song, he went out and met her.

"I guess we're going to have to have a truce," he told her. "The boy changes things, you'll admit."

"I do."

"Effie and you arranged it, I guess. His working here."

"I had nothing to do with it." She was meekly indignant. "Effie and Jay did the arranging. I was only told about it, like you."

"Would you have stopped it if you could?"

"I've thought about that. I don't think so. He's got to have something to do until schooldays if I'm to keep him. You can't coop a young thing up and expect it to stay." They avoided each other's eyes. Helen told him rather passionately, "No, I guess I would have tried to keep him away from you. And I thought Effie—" She stopped, but Jim heard her.

"She didn't want it, either?"

Helen Taylor shook her head. "But something changed her mind. Jay, I guess. Oh, he was curious about you! Babbled on like somebody, I don't know, in love." He saw her blush.

"That's a funny thing to say."

Grimly she told him, "It has happened. He's not like—" Rapidly, for her, she said, "He's a lot like Ludie."

"Are they kin?" They both looked shocked by the drift of the talk.

"Why, they're—" He held his breath. As curt as possible she told him, or asked him, "Isn't everybody kin in the South?" Laughing privately she said, "I know Effie and I call each other cousin. I'm probably kin to you, if the truth be known!" To emphasize the friendliness, she lifted her umbrella inviting him to step under out of the rain.

He shook his head at the offer. "I'm soaked through already," and sought to end the talk on a joking tone, "I hope it's not true about all of us being kin. That'd make Effie and me—"

She interrupted, laughing, "Incesters?"

"Is that the word? 'Incestuous,' ain't it, schoolmarm?"

"I think you're right. And yonder's Pone with the truck, as I live and breathe!" She took off, dipping her umbrella up and down and calling to Pone.

"Tell him to hold up, Helen. He's early." But he knew it

was not so. The fact was, he had lingered at breakfast for the first time in his life. Hitching up, another fact came to him, an omission that he supposed accounted for his shiver, and one that he knew had not been lost on Helen. He had not inquired about what must have been a rocky and perhaps dangerous ride into town yesterday, a ride that had included his wife as a passenger.

Jim and Jabez worked in the rain and the mud, resettling tilting rows of corn, cementing them in with globs of clayey earth. Jabez performed his part of the messy task with the glee of a child, his eyes bright and his color high. Jim kept glancing at the face under the too big hat, drawn by a combination of its vitality and the mystery of the degree of kinship between that face and Ludie's. He did not know if he had stopped Helen Taylor from telling him, or if she had stopped herself. He tried to recall the exact words leading up to the break, but could not. It would not be simple to ask the boy, and the longer he waited the more complicated it got. The time would have been yesterday when he could have asked a casual question without explaining more than that he had met her. And did he want to know? If not, why did he continue to worry it? He had always been direct, when directness would not come across as bad manners.

"You have much company, growing up?" he asked, lifting a hill of corn back into its crater while Jabez rooted around his feet, filling, and they both tamped with their brogans as cloddy and heavy as the base of the cornstalks.

"Too much, and not enough. According to my dad, I had too much."

"Big family, and he didn't want it?"

"We didn't have a big family. Just me." As Jim's breath was sliding quietly out Jabez added, "And a sister."

Jim worked at it but his breath was ragged and rough when he said, "Then there's not just you." He felt that Jabez was forcing him to wait before he said, "Now there is." He turned away from Jim to say, "Now there's not even me. There's just them, the way she wanted it. I'm here . . ." Jim gazed at the boy's back and had, once again, the sense that Jabez was distant and alone. "—and she's dead." Ashamed, Jim breathed easily.

"Your sister," Jim said. Jabez turned back, lip lifted in a snarl.

"Not the *other* one. Old Typhoid Mary. I wish she was."

"You could go back home then."

"And have my ass kicked? Not me!" He picked up a clod and threw it as far as he could, yelling, "Not me! Not me!"

"Whupped you, did he," Jim said and set back to work. "Reckon you earned it."

"Reckon I did," Jabez mocked. "Reckon every time he goes in that loft he wishes I was there to kick around. Reckon he'd like to tear that loft down."

"Guess I know what you're talking about. Me, I never got caught." Not doing *that,* he thought, as a large juicy apple, green and dappled pink, with one large bite missing, floated across his inner field of vision. He saw it, for the first time, for what it had been in the Biblical sense and wondered if that had not really been at the bottom of his father's reasoning, that had led to the one brutal beating he had ever given his oldest son. Jim was amazed to think that all the times he had pondered the circumstances and event of the beating, he had never before seen the apple in the light of Eden.

"My dad damn near killed me on account of a green apple." He thought the story would not do either of them any harm, and might do Jabez some good because the boy's face was flushed with his continuing anger. "Well, it was one apple finally did it, but it took a lot of them to get me there. Several summers' worth, point of fact."

Working comfortably, reliving his foolish days of youthful greed, he spun out the tale for Jabez.

"My dad thought green apples were fine if you cooked 'em in a pie or fried 'em, but he was certain sure they caused worms if you ate 'em raw. And I reckon our stomach-aches bore him out, but it didn't stop us."

When the three children were too small to be of much help on the farm and were free to roam through the days as they pleased—which meant to their father that they were free to eat green apples unchecked—at the end of each day the father would stalk around the orchard, looking for apple cores. He would gather the harvest into a pile and make each child claim his share, depending upon their honor not to have disposed of the cores, and on that basis he would calculate the probable number of worms in each small stomach. They were then dosed according to the worms each was presumed to house, with a mixture of castor oil and buckthorn syrup and santonica.

The ritual, the idea, the dosage cured Clara of her passion early on, and Will halfway through his third season, but Jim would have taken his worms straight if he could chase them with green apples liberally sprinkled with salt. His father even went so far as to blame Jim for leading his younger brother and sister down the apple path.

The result of his passion was a yearly feud between Jim and his father, which continued until Jim was ten. By then he was working in the fields alongside his father, but when the rest of the family napped at dinnertime Jim would go to the orchard and gorge on a full stomach, and later he would be sick in the hot sun. Even the humiliation of having the field hands watch him be childishly sick could not modify his addiction. Finally his father gave him a warning. It was given solemnly, in private, as befitted Jim's status as a full-time wage earner. The Cummins boys were paid for their labor, the same daily rate as the field hands, another family custom without precedent in the countryside. Jim saw the occasion as the potential turning point in their relationship. He believed that once his father had licked him, they could go back to their mutual respect. He had never been able to see his disobedience as a lack of respect for his father, but rather as the result of an obsession for which he paid in full by taking his medicine without protest.

Still, following the warning, he tried to see it as his father saw it, as a sign of disrespect, and kept away from the orchard. But he never could seem to get enough to eat, no matter how he stuffed at the table. He would wake up in the night with hunger pains much worse than the cramps he had got from the apples. One night close to midnight, nearly a week after their talk, Jim got out of bed and went downstairs and out to the orchard. He made no effort to be quiet in the house, no more than he would have done if he were only going for a drink of water. He climbed the first tree he came to and sat in the lowest notch, smelling the green lures dangling around him, waiting for his father. When he came soon afterward, hulking through the gate in his nightshirt, he and Jim regarded each other in the clear light of the moon.

Jim picked an apple. His father tore a switch from a peach-tree. Jim saw that his father had respected him by not anticipating his motive enough to bring with him a knife to cut the switch. He struggled with the tough slick young branch, tearing a long strip of bark away with it. Jim waited until his father was armed before he took a bite.

Jim could feel his flesh being torn away in strips by the sharp sticky switch, wet with sap and then with blood. His mother had tended him through the night. In spite of her remaining stony-faced and brusque throughout, Jim had suspected that her sympathy was with him, and because he did not want it, he managed to endure the treatment without making a sound. It had seemed to him that the night's business concerned only himself and his father, with Jim as his father's victim, but a boiling-down process over the years had revealed to him that he had been his own victim, the victim of his lust. He had been glad to make the discovery for it freed him of any ill feelings he might have held for his father. He thought that he had gone on rereading the incident as if it were a story for the pleasure of getting to the happy ending: the father freed of blame, the boy freed of hard feelings. But today the familiar story was extended by Jim's surprised thought that, by being forced to punish him, the father had been a victim of the boy's lust too. Looked at that way, it was plainly the boy who had manipulated the father all along!

For Jabez's benefit, he went further, saying that maybe a victim was not somebody who paid, as he had done, and as Jabez had done, but rather was somebody from whom something was extracted and nothing given in return. His father was no brute who enjoyed giving whippings. He had never whipped any of them until that night. So what had he gotten?

Then Will came into Jim's mind, and though he did not share the vision with Jabez, he could see Will standing at the foot of the bed, clinching and unclinching his fists, white as a sheet, and in the reliving, Jim believed that he could feel excitement coming from his brother.

To get shed of the picture, Jim said, "Hell, if a kid of mine used me like that, I'd kick his butt so high the bluebirds would nest in it."

Jabez laughed and said, "It wasn't like that with me. He said I wasn't manly." His smile became private. "Trouble was, I was too *manly*."

"How old *wuz* you?" Jim asked derisively, wanting to return to their old bantering, a tried and true defense against the unknown that the boy seemed to be conjuring up in his fields. In spite of the laughter, he believed that Jabez was working on the quick of the nerve, that the memory was like tearing away a hangnail.

"The last time was last year."

"If we were men at thirteen there wouldn't be any point to growing. We might as well keel over of old age around voting time." To defuse the seriousness that had happened in spite of him, and to divert Jabez, Jim gave his pants a clownish hitch. "Might be the salvation of the hull goddamned country, at that." But he could not rouse the boy out of his mood, which gave him a glassy-eyed and feverish look. Finally, gauging the passage of the morning as well as he could and worried, Jim told him, "Go on up to the house and dry off. I'll be up before long and rustle us up some grub."

The boy went without a protest, which bothered Jim, and he followed soon after. As he expected, he found Jabez fiddling with food, but his actions lacked force, and his color was too high to be blamed on the heat from the kerosene stove. Jim laid the back of his hand on Jabez' forehead and found the fever.

Saying "This is a fine hidy-do," he got Jabez undressed,

dried him off, and put him to bed, where he was instantly
asleep. By the time Jim had fed himself and cleaned his dishes
the rain had grown too heavy to allow any thought of work
outside. Feeling helpless, he set about doing what he imagined Effie did each day of her life to keep the place as spotless
as it always was. At daily work, did Effie burn the way he was
doing? and having thought it he realized that he too was
running a temperature. Visualizing the cisterns overflowing
with water he lit the heater in the bathroom and waited impatiently until he could have a tub bath. He asked himself if he
thought he could wash the fever away. If so, he should fetch
the boy in first and scrub him down and let the fever that
had burned Jim's hand run out the drain. He went into the
bedroom and looked at Jabez, who opened his eyes. His first
words to Jim gave information that he was in a dream, or
delirious.

"They were doing it to me. Billy and Amos and all the rest.
When he caught us Billy was on top. He pulled Billy off, and
it made a sound like a shoe coming out of mud. Everybody
called Billy 'stud' on account of his size. He was the oldest,
seventeen, and he was scared. He was the first one and I tried
to love him but he didn't want me to. Once he hit me when
I said I loved him and he stopped coming around until I didn't
care any more. By that time Amos and I—It wasn't the same,
though. I'd got used to Billy and I couldn't even feel Amos."

Jim tried on perplexity but it would not fit, like clothes he
had outgrown. What Jabez was talking about was what country boys called 'cornholing,' a practice that had gone on when
Jim was a boy, but one he had never been more than curious
about, knowing that it worked two ways and that you had to
submit before or after you had taken. The practitioners had
been oblique but they had gotten across the idea of the honor
system. When, in their code, they said to each other, "Finny
in a?" he would leave, or not join them when they left for
somebody's barn. When he or they had gone, the thought of
what they were going to do did not trouble him or color their
continuing relationships. Kids had to do it, that was all, and as
it worked out, their most potent years were given to each

other because society had set it up that way, as they set up all of life, with taboos and every kind of restrictive threat. When boys and girls finally came together they were no longer boys and girls but grown-up mysteries who never would understand each other. The men would stay together when they could, and the women would form opposing parties. The one time Miss Ethel had closed herself off from him was when he tried to talk to her, halting in speech, cracking his knuckles in nervousness, about what he saw as society's failure. He saw the two spots of color the size of quarters on her cheeks. "I have no connections," she said, "in that part of the country."

Years later, talking with Ludie about it, she had got the point he had missed, the point of Miss Ethel's wit. "What she meant was, below the equator," and Ludie had laughed and touched him on the crotch.

Looking down at the figure in the bed with some pity and some desire, Jim recalled the determined talks he and Ludie had had on the subject, because—Ludie's voice: "Men and women never talk about it, don't clear the air. Everybody takes for granted that they're supposed to be like that. But they aren't. *We're* not going to be enemies." She was forceful. "We're talking about it now. We know what we're up against." "I'm up against you," he said, "right where I belong." "Yes, oh yes." "Why can't we, then?" "You give me a precious ring, I give you one," and she hooted and hollered. But she meant it, and because she did not want to be a tease she would not let him touch and fondle her precious ring under her clothes, until he could go on and slip it on for keeps. But he could touch her elsewhere, while her hands on him, releasing him from his clothes, gave him what he had to have as often as they both could bear it.

The figure on the bed was quiet, eyes closed, long eyelashes resting far down the cheekbones. The tangled yellow-brown hair covered the pillow. Jim slipped his hand under the covers and cupped the bottom that was both hard and tender. The figure stirred, and the boy's voice said something. Jim withdrew his hand and looked at it, wondering what it would do if he said to it, as if it were a horse, "Giddy up." The hand trembled.

"Go forth and multiply and replenish the earth," Jabez said. "But they're two separate things. Multiply means have babies. Replenish the earth means die. What God meant was have babies and kill them. That way nothin's handed on." His voice was rational, but when he opened his eyes it took a while for him to bring Jim into focus. "We couldn't have babies. Safe." The word "safe" lingered and ran down and became rhythmical breathing.

Jim undressed and went naked to the bath where he ran a tub and hunched in it, too big to lie down and stretch out. He sluiced himself and soaped, watching his cock finally go under and stay under like a submarine on a mission. The cold rainy air through the open door was soothing and then invigorating. When he had let out the water and dried himself, he walked naked to the bedroom and got in bed.

He felt feverish still, but it had a clean feeling, like the distillation of all the emotions he had experienced in the past days but with the dregs removed and thrown away. What was left was a clear bright burning that lay on his skin like shellac with no penetrating powers. It was protective; nothing could get in and nothing could get out.

But a memory of another feverish time came weaseling in. As far as he knew, it had been the only other time he had run a fever since childhood. He was sitting at the table, Effie was dishing up food. Coming to him she had set the dish down and laid her hand on his brow, saying, "You don't look right to me." He moved her hand from his forehead to his lips. Effie pulled him around, intending to pet him. He recalled that he wanted to tell her something, and then it came: he had wanted to say that Will wouldn't leave him alone, that he had found in a jacket of Will's a paper in German with a word that frightened him, he could not say why. He could see the word behind his closed eyes: Lebensborn. Instead of telling her he leaned forward and pressed his head against the place where Effie's legs came together. Feeling her try to withdraw, he rubbed his head up and down, back and forth, with increasing hardness, holding her to him with a hand on each buttock. He felt her outrage begin in her apron, which shook with it like a high leaf on a tree. Her little hands pushed at his shoulders, too stiff with shock to use more than the heels. He looked down the future and knew that if she ever got up nerve enough to mention that day, and she might when they were eighty and safe, the word she would use to describe what she felt would be *mortified*. He knew he would let her get away with it, would not say that *mortify* meant denial and punishment, and what about the mortification of his own flesh, all his whole life long?

Jabez cried out, "You're closer to her than I am, you son of a bitch." Jim leaned over him, asking quietly, "Her?"

"Her. Her. All of 'em. Women. You're the real sissy. Too dumb to know it. I make fun but you love 'em. You're closer, see." He gritted his teeth, ground them with a rending sound. "I only loved *her*. She was like me." He gave a long laugh. "Crazy." He fell asleep, or out of his dream.

Jim watched him until his face swam and then lay back feeling the tide of warmth moving over his body like a hand. When it settled on his cock he felt that it was really a hand but did not check for dread of discovering it was only his own.

When he awoke it was past time to feed, water, and milk the cattle. It seemed to his testing hand that Jabez was considerably cooler, but he thought it might only be in contrast to his own burning. He knew if he could not manage to recover he would have to let Woody know, but he would not give in until he had to, to asking another man to do his chores. He put on pants and shoes without socks and an old weatherproof and did his work, pondering the fever. It could not be from poisoning on Huffines's canned goods, because the boy had thrown that out of his system and so would not be sick, and anyway, though there was dizziness, there was no nausea. He heard Jabez's answer to his question about what ailed the boy: "Deprivation," and startled the heifer with a huge guffaw. He told the heifer, "Fever's a cover-up for a lot of things, the way liquor is, but I'll be damned—"

His best bet would be to waylay Helen Taylor and get her to spend the night. She could cook for them, nurse them, and run errands, if it came to that. Sloshing through the odorous muck in the barnyard he added another category for her, one newly created by a mixture of current events, memory, and the mind set loose: chaperone. He found that "to name" was not "to purge" and wondered if Miss Ethel knew. But this was the part of the country where she had no connections. No, this was a country she did not know existed.

Helen Taylor's presence was cheery, marred only by the expression on her face when she saw evidence of their having shared the bed. It was a look devoid of charity or a grasp of the situation, which would have had one sick person toiling up the steps to check on another person equally sick. But the look had gone by without words to compound it, or clear it. It had lived on her face and then gone without another to replace it, followed only by blankness. Jim thought the blankness was like the expression a person wore who had not heard a thing you said because they did not want to.

"Chills and fever go together," was her explanation of the sickness. "You were shivering this morning, Jim Cummins, when we had our talk. I started to say something then, but just about that time I saw Pone drive up in the truck, and it clean went out of my head. As far as this one is concerned—" indicating Jabez, who was sitting up eating a bowl of soup— "he's as prone as I don't know what to bad colds. Mark my words, you'll both be fine by morning. And then, young sir," she said, not quite playfully, "I'll expect you to spend your nights where you are supposed to. The terms of your employment do not include a—" her eyes flickered—"a bed." She regretted something, Jim could see that, and the tone of her voice showed a wish to backtrack. "Not that I think you are not welcome. And not, Jim, that I would let you think for a minute's time that I am not grateful."

Jim waited, grinning slightly, and got what he had expected. "When I go to the wedding, as I have been requested to do, I will certainly thank you for having Jabez here." She faltered over his open grin that contained plenty of malice. "Effie said—" her defense began.

He rescued her. "Sure she did. I figgered you'd worked it

out before the ride was over." Topping her attempt to bridle he told her cheerfully, "Old Junie couldn't get hitched without you there."

"Well, I've always liked her," Helen lied.

She fed them tea and washed the dishes, giving them an anecdotal account of her day at the restaurant, voice raised to include Jabez, who had gone back to bed. When she had finished she said, "I suppose I'll go up now and make up our beds, Jay."

"I can stay here. Can't I, Jim?"

"Why, Jay," Helen said, "a man needs his bed to himself. Unless—" she gave Jim a coy look and shook her head, indicating that the sexual allusion should be left implicit because of the youth of the listener. He had an impulse to rub his crotch meaningfully at her but withstood it. "Besides, if Jim Cummins rolls over on you in the night he'll mash you into that mattress!"

"He didn't last night."

Jim did not want Helen Taylor's response, whatever it might be, and beat her to it by telling the unseen Jabez, "You can stay where you are, or you can go upstairs to a clean bed. This one's kind of sweaty now. But I don't see it as a problem either way." Through his fatigue he told her, "Beds upstairs are all made. Effie's the kind of woman changes and washes those clean sheets every week. Hope, I guess. Guess she hopes she'll have visitors. And now, by gum, she has. Don't you forget to tell her, Helen."

"I won't," Helen said, her tone making up for her enforced silence. Jabez giggled.

When Jabez had been led, grumbling, by his determined aunt to a clean bed, Jim stripped and got carefully between the sheets on his own side, avoiding contact with the warm hollow beside him as though Jabez occupied it still. But when he awoke in the night he found that he had filled the hollow with a pillow and lay on it, embracing it, in full, painful erection.

He got up and found Jabez' shirt—Effie's shirt—and took from the pocket the sack of tobacco and papers. For the first time since his drinking days he rolled a cigarette and sat in his chair smoking. His heart thudded when he heard the stairs creak, and his cock followed the stealthy descent, rising to meet it as though each step marked the progressive opening of a place that would receive him in his impressive and desirable fullness. He got up and walked to the kitchen door, and it was Helen Taylor he took into his arms, whose hand scrabbled for and found him and took his dimensions.

Only one man has ever been in me—man now, boy then. My own brother. I was not yet in my teens. A rainy morning. He, nine years old to my twelve, has crawled into my bed to wait for the call to breakfast and snuggle as he does each morning. We snuggle and tickle each other, rolling about to get the upper position. As usual I tickle him there, exploring. The little sac that I have to go easy on, and behind it the ridge, larger today, that connects back and front. To him it is only a game but to me it is business, having to do with my future, my fate. Getting down to business means that my hand settles on his bottom and then retraces its old path until it comes to the appendage that is sometimes soft, sometimes firm. Today it is as hard as a bone; my fingers can feel veins. I notice then that he is lying quiet, and it frightens me at first and then stirs me to know that he knows it is no longer a game. With my help he gets on top of me, and we put it in.

Returning to Jim's arms where she leans, holding Effie's Cross in her hands—returning from the rainy morning forty years ago to the rainy night and the kitchen door against which Jim pushes her—she feels in her organs the outrage of her brother's thing in her and the burning that had gone on for days and the shame of the blood on the sheet that she had tried to hide from her mother, who had only said, "You're early. I was, too." In comparison, her brother had been like a needle to Jim's—she doesn't know what—*turkey baster*, she thinks in triumph. She reaches for his bags, as Effie calls them, and thinks as Effie had on her wedding night, though Effie had screamed it out—"Bull."

Even as Jim prepares to ram her against the wall and fuck

her there, he feels the rejection rising in her, hears in her breathing not desire but panic, which he has learned to read as easily as any book. His cunning rescues him, working for him without his help.

"Come on to bed," he says, "Effie. Come on, Ef," and something in him produces tears to mark his painful frustration, to go with the play acting. The ache in his groin is real. "I want to, Ef. It's been so long. Jesus, I'm hurtin. Come on."

Helen Taylor's impulse is to hold on, to tell him, mimicking Effie's voice, "All right, honey, but get The Thing first." What had Effie called it? "Get Short Pecker, honey." She wonders if her piteous cries could be more awful to hear than this man's alien need, the first time she has heard it given voice. It is like the Call of the Wild, with snow under and around it. It could freeze a woman's marrow. Or loosen her bowels. Ludie, calling his name. Soiled the bed. Said it was Jim's baby. Did that happen? The possibility that it had makes her drop the cock and with it her last chance.

"It's Helen, Jim," she said, moving away. "You're walking in your sleep. I heard you get up and thought you might be sick." She repeated, "It's Helen," to re-establish her identity. Negotiating the black stairs she had named herself otherwise: *Nightcrawler*.

Hearing Jabez at the top of the stairs, thinking that her sneakiness was probably worse than his because it was said he only listened, she called up to him angrily to *get back in bed*. She tried to modify it with explanation, "Jim's feeling poorly."

Jabez lay awake hating his aunt with a hatred that could easily have let him murder her. He could see her hair matted with blood on the pillow and the thick gluey seepage that continued from the hatchet wound in her skull. She had tried to tuck him in, bending in a motherly parody over him in the lamplight, her dissembling features twisted out of shape with attempted tenderness. To him she looked like the witch in "Hansel and Gretel," coming in the night to test his fatness. He had given her arm a whack that he knew would leave a bruise, and he longed for the morning when he could inspect his handiwork. Until she came he had thought that this would be his wedding night. Both Jim and himself burning had seemed to him symbolical. He knew that he was lovesick, whatever Jim thought the illness, his or Jabez's, was. Their two days and one night together with only a touch here and there—Jim's hand on his hip last night; Jim on top of him when they wrestled—was the real cause of their fever. His effort and success in making Jim the pursuer had drained him, too. It was a lesson he had learned well at the hands of Billy Taylor: there were the hunters and there was the quarry. He was a hunter but had learned how to conceal it, for when a hunter came after another hunter, one of them had to play a role. He had hunted Jim until Jim caught him, or so it would have been if his witchy old aunt hadn't stuck her nose in.

Hearing his aunt creep downstairs he knew that she was going to try to get Jim for herself. Nothing ever said, no proof ever offered, could change his mind about that. He knew how women lied to themselves to cover their motivations, all of them except Ludie, who was what she was and no copy. All his life he had watched his mother leading his father on, then covering up her wanting with delay. Just before he left, or was thrown out, he had made them watch a one-man show in which he had given a perfect imitation of his mother heating his father up and then pretending that she couldn't go to bed just yet because she had forgotten to do something imperative like straighting the goddamned doilies, and he had sashayed around, twitching his behind luringly, watching his father over his shoulder. This had led to a terminal scene, as it turned out, that Ludie would have enjoyed.

Hearing his aunt creep-creeping down the stairs he followed, matching his footsteps to hers, and thought that if she turned around and saw him, billowy in his big nightgown, she would die of a heart attack and his troubles would be over. He would go on down the stairs, stepping over her, and into Jim's bed where he belonged. He had laid claim to that bed that could never again be Jim and Effie's. It was Jim and

Jabez's now. People could call them "the two J's" or just "JJ": "I'm going to JJ's tonight."

From the top of the stairs he heard the silence and then the heavy breathing and then Jim's voice so close that he almost bolted, imagining as he had his aunt's crablike progress toward the bed. In his mind he had seen her crouching beside the bed, her hand snaking under the covers, rooting for Jim's root. When Jim felt his ass today it had been without any stealth, and Jabez could have claimed him then, but he had not wanted a wedding afternoon, for which an expression did not exist; he wanted what was his expectation and right, as traditional as any bride cleft in both places. That he was a real man in front would be no hurdle at all after a few times, for from that very satisfactory spout could come the evidence of his joy, a gift for Jim that he would come to see as a lot better than the secretive and unprovable satisfaction that a woman had to offer or conceal. How many times had he heard his father plead, "Did you honey?" because all of his humping and groaning had not produced anything to show for it! "Did you?" No question would be needed from Jim, no answer from Jabez, to prove how good Jim had been as a lover.

He heard his aunt's lying words explaining her lurking downstairs, shifted his weight to relieve cramped muscles, and got her shrieking response. The fury in her voice told him all that he might have needed to know.

When morning came Jabez told his aunt, "I'm too sick to get up." She tried to look sympathetic and failed when he added, "'cept maybe to go to the bed downstairs."

Sweetly she said, "Then I'll be back tonight to tend you and stay over."

"It may be too late by then."

"Dying, are you?" Her face said she almost wished he would. She became thoughtful. "I suppose I could take the day off."

"How'll you let them know? There's no telephone in working order anywhere, not even in Salvation." Vaguely he added, "Jim said Woody Barnes or somebody told him."

"Pone can drive me in and I'll tell them, and he can drive me back out." She sounded as though she had made up her mind. He called her bluff.

"You'd have to go with him on the milk route. Corinth and Providence and Middletown, all the way to Miss Effie's." He smiled. "Miss Effie's mama's. You might get back here by four o'clock if you're lucky."

She exploded mildly. "If *I'm* lucky? And me willing to take the day off and miss my pay, *and* my tips, to look after you. Why Jabez, I honestly didn't know you could be so ungenerous!"

Impatiently he rejected her sentimental try at blackmail. He was not about to feel sorry or say that he did. "Is Jim all right?"

She told him sullenly, "Off to the barn. Expecting his breakfast, I daresay."

"Then—dear—he can look after me if I need it," and he gave her his lopsided kid smile that had never failed to win her. "Look at me," the grin said, "I'm just a kid. Cranky 'cause I'm sick, sall." And the altered expression in his eyes said, "You're scaring me just a little with all these undertones. I've played for fun, but now it's gone and got too grown-up for me." The quivering cheek and rapidly blinking eye and suddenly lost mouth—he had turned in profile and so only had to manipulate the one side—threatened to say, out loud, "I want my mama!"

She sighed, smoothed the counterpane. "Oh, Jay dear, you're right. I'd probably get fired." Pensively, she worked out her release, vaguely copying gestures recalled from movies seen in girlhood. "*Then* what would we do? How *would* we manage?" Her fingers pleated the sheet. Jabez smiled, reading her: two orphans outside a closed door. Knowing she could not read him, he thought, I'm inside, you're out.

She went out, closing the door behind her, which he promptly opened when the stairs had creaked on the bottom step.

He expected to hear from the kitchen some admission, if only by omission, of what had gone on last night. His imagination, which did not need fever to make it overheated, and especially not in the circumstances, had supplied scenes to account for last night's heavy breathing, that had preceded Jim's words, "I want to, come on." He had seen his aunt kneeling in front of Jim, her teeth out, sucking—something he had never done, so he had not lied to Jim about that. He read, though, and knew that it was a technique he would eventually have to learn to be sexually well rounded. But it could only amount to a preliminary, "foreplay," as the sex books called it, for what satisfaction could there be in the long run for the one doing the sucking? Jabez had never sucked on a tongue, either. The boys would have killed him for suggesting it. But in his mind he had become accomplished at French kissing, and saw the two things as pretty much the same: as leading up to the act of penetration, for which Oscar Wilde had been condemned. It was plain to him from his reading that Oscar had buggered Bosey, but had he ever turned over or lifted his legs for any of the ragamuffins he slummed with, had he ever taken them into the mouth that could make pearls out of common words, and made their probably dirty cocks pearly, too? Jabez thought that he himself was cynical enough, or practical enough, which in sex was the same thing, to forget about fastidiousness under the circumstances, as Oscar must have done. But practical consideration made him consider the role of teeth, and it was helpful to his fantasy, which would have got hung up there, to give his aunt removable teeth, though her own were real and handsome, her best feature, which accounted for her nearly incessant smile.

Jim came in and there was talk, none of it too revealing. Their constraint was that of people who did not like each other. Jim thanked Helen for cooking for him, apologized for the need, saying there now was no further need, for he felt fine. He told her not to worry about old Jay because he would look after him as if he was his own—and he stopped. Helen murmured something he could not hear and was silent. Jabez, in an experiment that had him peer into her brain and find the thoughts there like bacteria under a microscope, had her say, "As if he was your own son?" and Jim, cleverer than she, said, "I reckon I was going to say kin, Helen." Jabez cheered his cunning, because husband and wife were kin, closer than relatives. His hand clawed at the sheets when he imagined Helen's response: "Flesh and blood?" and felt himself hanging by a thread as fine as a spider's, waiting for Jim's answer to occur to him.

What Jim actually said was, "There's the milk truck. You better scoot," and Jabez breathed easily, thinking he could not have done better himself.

Jabez went to the window and watched through the apertures of lashing tree limbs as his aunt climbed into the truck, her skirt riding up to show the way she had knotted the tops of her stockings instead of wearing garters. Her fat knees and the dented flesh at the stocking tops gave him a twinge of feeling for her as sharp as a splinter under a fingernail.

The sight was as dry and unlubricious as the smell of chair cushions where aging unmarried women had sat. Smelling the cushions when his mother's visitors would have gone, his mother at the door with them saying good-by so that the cushions were just abandoned and still warm, the small boy had not found what he expected, which was a smell of bottoms or of washed or unwashed flesh. His mother's cushion smelled both dirty and perfumed, but the other ladies had left a smell not to be compared with anything else that had an odor. All he could compare it to was a kind of expression sometimes seen in church on Mother's Day. It was the look of old women wearing white instead of red roses, which showed that their own mothers were dead. As an older boy able to make connections, he had concluded that the cushion smell was a kind of signal like the white rose, a message of bereavement left there, hopelessly, because who but small boys sniffed cushions and received the message? It would be like an animal in rut leaving in the corner of a cage, into which another animal never came, a cry for help in pee.

Jabez watched Pone swing the milk cans onto the truck and then turn as though he had been called. He saw his aunt face the house, too, and he joined her, became part of her vision, waiting for Jim to appear. What did she see, to give her such an expression? A man, a big man, something denied her, something she denied? A thing she feared. Was it *the thing* she was afraid of or what it stood for—the whip of the slavemaster? The pain caused by the whip could be stood, could be worked, like a bright but ugly scrap, into the pattern of a life; but the right of another person to use the whip on you named a condition that could be unbearable, named you: victim.

In the town there were girls, pretty girls, not just the dogs, who were marked for spinsters. Some of those whose cushions he had smelled had been more than pretty, had been lovely. But without knowing it they gave off an odor that kept men away. Maybe it was the smell of somebody who would be victimized by union with another person. Were some, like Effie, able to deceive and manage enticement in spite of no personal charms, or did some men, like Jim, have lousy smellers? Jabez had stood on street corners watching the parade of girls, pearls and cashmere sweaters, pleated skirts swinging jauntily, and picked out the ones doomed to the lonely cushion. His sense of smell was tremendous, because he was so opposite to girls. But Jim, loving them, was closer to them and would be inclined to charity or a willful ignorance, giving them the same benefit of the doubt that he would give himself.

Jim came into view, and Jabez looked at him with his own eyes, seeing beneath the baggy clothes the body that carried no excess weight, whatever Effie and others like her might think. Starting with the big head of curly hair under the roughrider hat that Jim wore rakishly, Jabez drew the outline of his man on the pane: the big neck with tendons too rigid, the shoulders like fields with deep hollows near the neck that could hold a quart of water each, the muscled arms that, in his aunt's eyes, must represent brutality. Jabez had studied Jim's back by lightning, tracing its deep undulations where it curved like riverbanks down to the bed of his spine. When he was tickled in his sleep Jim had flopped over and presented his front for inspection, anticipating the storm such a revelation would create by his snores like mountain thunder. Resolutely Jabez stuck to his lover's back and traced on down the body to the hips and the ass as hard as granite: the center of force that scared Effie to death, for to fight it would be like fighting against the thrust of one of the knobs that surrounded the valley. When, naked, Jim stretched, cords stood out in his legs, and his bunched calves, sliding up, were like animals moving toward birth. Inside his muddy brogans were muscular feet with big toes larger than some dicks, and Jabez was not thinking about babies'.

And inside the outline, the raw muscles swimming in blood. Too near the surface. What muscles women had were buried in softness, safe under cushions, and their sex was protected inside, but men went around exposed, no place to hide, except in women; and to women like Effie and his aunt, a man must seem like a walking weapon, a knife without a scabbard, both the cause and the wound.

The truck pulled away and Jim turned about. His first glance found Jabez's window and a glimpse of Jabez's retreating face. Jabez saw the beginning of Jim's grin.

"How you feelin, ole hoss?"

"Nasty. Could I have a bath in the tub?"

"Boy, I'm right glad you brought that subject up." Jim reached for the kitchen matches and had to fumble the box to keep it from falling and spilling. "Got to fire up the boiler. Won't be long though. Feller like you don't use more'n a teacup full a water."

"That wouldn't clean my—" Jabez substituted "ear" for "ass" at the last minute, handing the ball to Jim. He asked, "Are you feeling all right now?" setting the strangeness of formality between them. Jim studied him.

"I'm ready as a firecracker." He struck a match. The lighted head broke off and rode a self-made arc to the linoleum, leaving a strong smell of sulfur, and of burnt linseed oil.

Jabez came out of the bathroom dressed and heard the crackling of wood and saw the pattern of the flames on the carpet. Jim was stretched out in his chair, his shoeless feet in rayon socks propped on the fender. He had on a broadcloth shirt and a pair of dark flannel pants. A belt of braided leather clasped against his belly a large buckle of polished brass with some kind of raised device on it. Giving it the once-over by firelight, Jabez would have settled for its being an ear of corn but did a double take when Jim said, flat and brutal, "My fuck belt," and Jabez saw that the device was a cock and balls, the balls appearing to be a pair of leaves. The rigid coldness of the brass genitals frightened him. There would be no give and take with such a thing. It would withdraw with innards stuck to its tip, the way a tongue adhered to cold iron. The ridges that Jabez had mistaken for kernels of corn were warts. He retreated to his side of the fire, thinking it was foreign territory and wondering how he had got there.

Jim's tone of voice had no friendliness in it. It had an inner repugnance that certain inevitable words were built around, words having to do with news of death, of craziness, of dangerous operations that would have to be performed. The words were spoken fastidiously, as though a clinical attitude could keep them from touching what they surrounded.

"I got this buckle at a carnival. Shot for it or pitched for it, I don't recall. They named it "the mystery prize," and everybody was going for it, girls and women too. Some rumor said it was mink step-ins, another one said it was a New Testament signed by Jesus Christ. Something for everybody. The Holy were in there pitching alongside the damned. The carnie running the operation guaranteed that it was something everybody could use, and when somebody said, "What if I already got one?" the answer was, "You can always use more of *this* thing." When it fell to me to win it everybody crowded around, but I saw right off what it was and stuck it in my pocket, telling them it was just a belt buckle and a gyp to boot. Some mystery prize, aye. People want what they don't understand, don't want what's plain. Unless they can get a ban against it, get it declared illegal or unreligious or some shit like that. Me too. I go around wanting something I could've had, that's shut away now as surely as if it was behind the Pearly Gates." He put his hand between his legs, caught up the weight there and held on. "Effie, who's got this legal, would give up her chance in heaven to be shed of it. One person I knew in this world wanted it. Two, now. You want it, don't you. Sometimes she looked no more than your age, did the last time I saw her. She wanted it so much it drove her crazy. What's it doing to you, boy."

It was not a question, and Jabez did not try to answer. Jim rolled a ball of spit around in his mouth and let fly at the fire. The contempt froze Jabez, as did the sound of the wind hanging on the shoulder of the house. Under Jim's words was something worse than curses, which he heard echoed in the wind. It was the kind of obscene murmuring that he could imagine a diseased woman doing at the ear of her victim. He could smell medicine, a smell like iodine.

Instead of scrouging back in his chair as he wanted to do, Jabez got up and went to the fire and gave a kick to a log. Behind him he could envisage the brass cock poised to enter him, and he drew in his butt, then quickly turned to see if Jim had read enticement into the movement.

"You, too?" Jim said, and in one movement circled the boy's waist and pulled him back and down, placing the crack of the struggling ass precisely on his erection. "We got a fire, a bed, I dressed in my Sunday clothes. Only one ceremony left, and that's the blooding."

Far down the wagon road Jabez thought that he could still hear Jim roaring as he had when Jabez made a run for it. He turned to face the house, running backward, until he fell sprawling on his back in a puddle full enough to drench him to the skin. The icy water shocked him out of the nightmare he had been in and brought his practicality to his rescue. He saw his aunt's house, the empty grate, the distant coal pile. He had been sick. The sickness would turn into pneumonia. He would die.

He walked into Jim's house, into the bathroom, took off all his clothes, took two towels, and went in to the fireside where he rubbed himself down in front of Jim as unconcerned as he had been yesterday and the day before. Deliberately he showed his front as well as his back to Jim, let Jim know that he was not a freak, something half man, half woman. If Jim shot or pitched for him now it would not be for another mystery package.

Squatting with his back to the fire, vigorously drying his long hair, he asked, "Did any girls ever see that buckle?"

Jim shook his head. "Never noticed it, anyway. Just one ever opened it."

"The one that wanted—"

"No. Just a one-shot." He amended it. "A no-shot."

Jabez peered up from under his hair and heard the sound of Jim's breath leaving him and watched the changes occur in Jim's face: hope and superstition seemed to go together, and turmoil. In alarm he called out, "Jim, what's the matter!"

Jim said, "I don't want to know. I don't want to know." He got up. Jabez watched him as he slowly unbuttoned his shirt, the sleeve cuffs first. The hand traveling down the row of front buttons could have belonged to a man in a trance. When the hand reached the belt it tugged the shirttails out and traveled on down to the last button. It waited then, the shirt swinging open on the terrible brass cock. Jabez took a forward step and opened the belt and the buttons on the fly. Jim was not wearing underwear and soon they were both naked, and soon afterward they were in the bed.

They lay as equals in the firelight, on their sides facing, and Jabez, for all the solemnity of the waited-for moment, found a place for the thought: I'm glad we weren't in the parlor. He could see them as they would have been, having to negotiate the chilly dining room, skirting table and chairs, sex and the thought of food in uncomfortable companionship. Coming into the bedroom from the dining room they would feel full by association and would wonder if sex should not wait until dinner had had time to digest.

Not yet aroused, Jabez gave Jim a calculated look, a duplicate of the one that had caused him to undress without a word, and sank deeply into relief as Jim moved over him, and then like a boy on a trampoline, he lifted from the comfort of footing however unsure and rose into the wildness of the known-unknown element above him.

Jim sank and sank, aware of expected obstacles giving way beneath him, as they should, but without wounds or sounds of hurt, which threw him further into a dream that had begun by the fireside with the familiar face peering from the cloudy hair. It took all of his senses including his fingertips to determine that he was finally fully contained and could move as he chose without apprehension like a blind man in rooms whose every object had been place by himself. He gave and received, and the motions of giving and taking had a naturalness allied to nature: one beast in a field without dimensions to inhibit it. His eyes were closed, but hearing, or thinking he heard, the words, "Feed me!" he responded to the old lure and looked. Nothing he saw changed his pleasure. The eyes beneath his own were ageless and sexless. He wondered how much he too had changed, and the eyes told him, better than a mirror could, what he was like *now,* someone without a past or a future. That a future existed toward which he and the eyes worked was hinted at by signaled panic which said *not yet,* but the eyes returned him to present instruction, a course in pleasure in which he learned about rhythm and about the eye of the storm in which nothing should happen except barely perceptible motion, when the sense of havoc around them brought the most excruciating joy. He could feel the network of his body and could think of it variously, in terms of the word itself: an irrigation system carrying his delight and fear, and a chain of radio stations broadcasting himself to himself. Miss Ethel was there with the word, and Ludie was there with the shocking release. His eyes closed; he cried out her name, or thought he did, but the sound another made covered it.

As though he were coming on his own stomach as well as inside someone, he felt inner spasms timed perfectly to his own and spurting outward results. He opened his eyes and looked at Jabez. The boy, like Ludie, was full of juice.

It was as if something he owed women, Ludie foremost, had been paid, and his debt was now to Jabez. In the course of an afternoon of repetitions that seemed, by their numbers and intensity, to cancel out the deprived past, Jim did not call out, nor conjure, another's name.

They lay in bed smoking, listening to the popping of the bark on the new log Jim had thrown on the fire. Jim lay waiting for remorse to strike.

Jabez asked, "Why did you try to scare me away?" As Jim said, "Try? Now I think I succeeded pretty damn good," he was thinking that his remorse had come before the event. Its last-ditch attempt had been in the effort—not conscious; he saw remorse working on its own—to stave off what had happened. What had to happen, he knew, as he had thought he understood earlier when he prepared himself, built the fire, changed the sheets on the bed while Jabez got ready.

He had been through it all in his mind the night before, saw where he was headed, where curiosity and need were pushing him. He had tried then, during the night after Helen had gone back up, to think of Jabez as a child, as jail bait, a representative of the all but nameless sins the Bible and the laws hinted at, as being worse than death, and had looked square at some of the consequences. Yet, for all that, he had come up against a stubborn streak that argued, with plenty of power, that he would only be taking what was not just offered but thrust on him which ever way he turned: by Effie's peculiar reluctance like lies; by Helen's morbid hints, and by Jabez, complete with words said in a dream or delirium as proof of how much he wanted and aimed to have what Jim alone had to give.

He had seen himself covered with slime, as filthy a specimen as could be dragged up from hell—a child polluter—but the stubborn voice asked, "Who's this polluter you're talking about?" and Jabez tracking him through the weeks crossed his brain. Jim had experienced wanting, and knew the real thing when he saw it, and knew it was need, too. He remembered himself at Jabez's age, on fire day and night with nothing he was willing to accept to quench the burning. Why? Because it was against the goddamned Bible, against all the goddamned laws, for all he knew, for a young thing to want that kind of relief. He saw Jabez as the same kind of victim he had been all his life.

Finally the argumentative voice brought the matter home. "Just a benefactor, are you now? Everybody else is to blame but you." The voice was disgusted. "How many chances have you had, and how many are you going to have? The kid says he can take it all, all of it."

Talking to Helen at the breakfast table, he had known—though not the exact time; Jabez's health would determine that—that he was going to fuck the hell out of her nephew.

"Did, too," he said aloud, and to Jabez's inquiring face after his long silence, he said, "Scared you."

Jabez put out his cigarette. "You talked crazy. I think you were scared of *me*." He tucked the top of his head in Jim's armpit, yawning into Jim's side. Jim did not like the tenderness or the assumption that it was returned, but when Jabez said, "Wake me if you want me," he could have seen by lifting the covers how much effect the words had. But to Jim's amazement the last word ended on a snore.

It was Jabez who woke Jim by slapping his erect cock against Jim's face. When Jim came fully to, it was to see a large male organ poised over his mouth.

He knocked Jabez to the foot of the bed and followed him there, feeling that the flood to his brain of all the blood in his body was lifting him up. His neck swelled until he could not get his breath. With the heel of one hand he pushed Jabez's chin up and back and with the other made a fist like a boulder, knowing the delivered blow would finish the boy off. His heart was making such a racket that he thought it was trying to tear a hole in his chest, trying to get out and beat Jabez to death. He knew he would kill the boy but did not know how. He knew it was a matter now of who survived, for to let Jabez live on was to become what he was. Jim, triumphant, told himself that he was a survivor, would outlive them all. He heard the boy's ragged efforts to breathe and thought such a death without scars, strangling without marks on the neck, could be blamed on his sickness of colds and fever. The boulder-hand regretted that it would not be allowed to land one killing blow in the hollow under the ribs. The hand seemed to be sobbing, "The son of a bitch." With a feeling of craziness, Jim looked at the hand, and as he did so, the paw under Jabez's chin relaxed its pressure. He towered over Jabez but felt himself to be in ambush, watching for the least movement to bring him out. There was none. After a time he realized that it was all over, and then saw that it was not yet done, though Jabez had given himself up for dead.

He had seen the sight all of his life, in animals and once in a person: a film formed on the eye, the coat or feathers or skin dulled as you watched, the muscles gave way, the creature would shit or piss. Before he saw it, he smelled that Jabez was no exception. If it had not been for the odor, he would have thought that Jabez had bled on the sheet, was bleeding, for the thin watery stuff leaked out as Jim looked.

Moving slowly, so as not to frighten him further, Jim got up and went to the bathroom where he splashed his head and neck with cold water, then wet a towel and brought it back and mopped up under the boy, who had not changed position.

Midway in his ministrations Jim felt something in him break, a membrane or a sac of fluid. He pulled Jabez's head to his belly and held it there, stroking the boy's hair and cheek and brow. After a time it seemed to him that his fingertips could sense the returning life, or the belief in life, which was what Jabez had let hold of. Jim's brother Will flung into his head as though sent there by a catapult. He stood there defiantly in such hard belligerence that his image seemed to have been painted on a stone. Aloud Jim said, as though Jabez could help him, "What am I going to make out of this? Didn't he go because of *believing* in something? If he had given up, why did he go away to die?"

He turned Jabez loose and went to the fireside, what was left of it, and began to dress. Half clothed, he saw that he was putting back on his Sunday gear and stripped again. He was reluctant to look at Jabez and risk seeing fear that he was coming after him again, to kill him or fuck him, which might now be the same thing. But because it was necessary medicine he took it without showing his feelings and, standing naked, turned and gave Jabez a full look. What he saw was something altered by him, but not visibly maimed. Jabez's eyes were calm and distant; he was still returning and seemed not to be sorry to make the trip. He certainly was not afraid. One hand was stroking his neck, and though he stopped doing it when

Jim looked at him, it was not done abruptly, nor did it continue long enough to make a point. The stroking tapered off, the hand moved down, unself-consciously giving a pat and a lift to the offending organ. Jim went over and took it in his hand and looked at it carefully. It was well made, and he was glad for Jabez. He tried to imagine the time when he could be aroused by it and could not. It was the first cock other than his own that he had ever touched. He thought how strange it must be for a girl. At least he knew what not to do, and his hand gently took the sac and handled it properly, recalling convulsive grips on his own that had sent him through the roofs of cars.

He returned the boy to himself and went to fetch his farm clothes. When he came back Jabez had stripped the bed and was standing naked in front of the built-up fire, warming his behind.

"I haven't got a stitch to put on," he said, "not even a pair of socks." Both accepted that his wearing anything of Effie's was now out of the question.

"You staying here tonight?"

"I better go on back and give the old girl a thrill."

Jim nodded. "Back 'fore long. Wrap up in a blanket." He set out for the tenant house. It was dark and cold, no more than fifty degrees, he estimated. He wondered what new calamity was in store, for him or the world. From a distance his big pond looked like a sea with the wind-thrown waves nearly touching the road. Skirting the pond he saw that when the waves moved back their maws were crammed with mud. He thought that they looked like children eating peanut butter. The image was cut into by another of Jabez's body oozing blood-brown onto the bed.

In Jabez's room he found the usual chaos, clothes flung every which way on the floor, from which he could take his pick. Among the jeans and tee shirts were a woman's slip and stockings, a pair of shoes, a bracelet. The bracelet was blue stones in imitation silver. He knew it well, had rubbed his cheek against it and the arm that wore it while he drove, a happy captive within the loop of that arm. Always when they stopped she would make a show of taking his handkerchief and pretending to wipe the green from the bracelet off his face. Were the slip, the stockings, the shoes, hers too? No, they were scaled for a lummox, for Helen. His girl could have worn the princess slip for a winding sheet.

With a hand that felt numb he scrabbled through the stuff on Jabez's dresser, a feminine, home-made thing of orange crates draped with cretonne. His breathing evened out. That was it. This had been Ludie's room, she had left the bracelet here. The boy, like a magpie, had been attracted to the color and brought it out into his nest.

In a notebook he found:

IN THE POTTER'S HOUSE, vessels are speaking.

Then said another, "Surely not in vain
My substance from the common earth was ta'en
That he who subtly wrought me into shape
Should stamp me back to common earth again."

Another said, "Why, ne'er a peevish Boy
Would break the bowl from which he drank in joy;
Should he that made the vessel in pure joy
And fancy, in an after rage destroy!"

Joy had been crossed out and *hate* written above it. He pondered the substitution which was like a written order that he had nearly filled. "Who are you, boy?" he asked and flipped through the pages. One sheet was covered with a name. Ludie, Ludie, Ludie. In fancy penmanship, in plain, in printing. Ludie.

Helen Taylor stood in the bedroom wearing her coat and hat. With her umbrella she pointed to the pile of sheets, letting the tip hover above the bloody-looking soiled part. A stamping upstairs sounded like a wild beast, and something crashed.

"The drought is over," Jim said.

Helen looked surprised, as though she had not known. "Why, I guess it is. There's mud everywhere." She looked down the pointer of her umbrella. "Somebody put his muddy shoes on the bed."

"A little mishap. No harm done." Upstairs something hurled against a wall. It sounded like Jabez. Jim felt that to keep talking was the thing. "I think the boy's going to be just fine."

Helen's continued surprise was like rouge and lipstick put on in a hurry without looking into a mirror; it did not match her face. She seemed to be embarrassed by his close attention and tried to redirect it. As though the solution were God-sent she smiled a little as she shook the point of the umbrella at the dirty sheets, leading them back to where they had been. Jim thought: That's her ace in the hole, and nearly sniggered.

Bashful, a little apologetic, she asked him, "What was he doing down the road, to fall in a mud puddle?" Her right to ask, and Jim's silence, encouraged a more righteous tone. "As sick as he was, Jim!"

Apparently to himself he said, "You thought he was bluffing, this morning." He remembered her. "Excuse me. You asked—?"

"What he was doing *down the road*."

"I guess you asked him that?" He pointed upstairs to the results of her prying, a Tarzanlike yodel of rage.

"He said you scared him."

"Truthful boy. Somebody brought him up good. Did he say how?"

Her eyes flickered. "Well, I didn't ask."

"Afraid he'd lie?"

"Maybe." Jim received the unspoken revision and answered it.

"But you'd like the truth, now."

She was very gentle. "It's always better to know. Children—" she emphasized the word—"hide things for a lot of reasons. But as his guardian—" she bore down—"I'm naturally concerned." He watched her find a train of thought that would lead back to her ace. "He must have misbehaved for you to have to scare him." She laughed. "I think you found him lying on the bed with muddy shoes and ripped in to him! Am I right?" She invited him over to her side, to a conspiracy. "Oh, I won't punish him, I promise you. You've already done that!" But he refused her by keeping still, and she requited him with a tone of voice so sly in its calm speculation that he felt his skin harden into armor. "Or is it you soils your clean sheets? These sheets were put on this bed since I left here. The pillows are still starchy. One pillow. The other looks . . . *used*."

Jim saw that Jabez had not removed the pillow cases. To eyes looking for it the imprint of the boy's behind could be made out of the indentation in the goosedown.

He attacked. "The others were kind of sweaty. You'll recall. Naw, damn, you didn't make it to the bed last night."

"Somebody else did, though!"

"Not last night." Logically he said, "I reckon if you come in and find an unmade bed and a naked boy, there's not much doubt about anything, is there?"

He hoped she would go on and act on that *anything*. Much later he told himself that he would have confessed if she had.

But she was puzzled. "I guess he was down here for the fire. Of course, there's a fireplace in his room, too. But that's unnecessary work for you, and you poorly. This morning I started to ask if I could build him a fire. But didn't."

"Thinking about me."

She was vague. "Well. But I was worried, and when I got to town I couldn't get it off my mind. It seemed like I was shirking my responsibilities. Him sick, and me there—"

At breakfast she had assured Jim that Jabez was bluffing. He had reminded her of this once but she had not agreed and now was working up a case based on that lack. He was drawn to help her out.

"Something send you a message on the drums that he was sickening?"

She turned fiery red. "I didn't even want to go this morning and you know it!"

"Maybe you hadn't ought."

"My thought exactly, Mr. Cummins!" She gave the sheets a vicious poke. "Mud, blood, or the other stuff. Which is it?"

Jim thought: She's summed us up, the whole human race. Mud, blood, or shit. Take your pick.

But it was as though she had not said a word about the substances. She went on with her story as though it had not been broken into by the practical question. To his bemusement she laughed.

"Pone told me old man Johnson was up before the court today. It appears that the Weidermanns—he's treated them like enemy aliens since the War, as everybody knows, and their family here as long as his if not longer—seems that they found out he was hoarding, and broke in there with witnesses and all, and made themselves quite a case. So Judge Wade was hearing them today. And sure enough, when we got into town there all those neighbors' automobiles were, lined up side by side on the square. I'm ashamed to say that I thought about the choice of rides out and not about their shameful business at all! Well, I'm a coward and I called up the restaurant, right there across the street! and said I had to tend my ailing nephew. But I had to lay low. Millie Simpson, the records clerk, is my friend, and so I went in there, swore her to secrecy, and amused myself the best way I could by looking up old trials. Everything is there, going back to when this state was a part of Virginia. Every misdemeanor, felony, malfeasance—a lot of that. That courthouse I was sitting in was built on graft." She shivered. "And so much *unnatural* conduct." Her eyes implored him. "You know that hamlet on the other side of Prices's Mill called Lickskillet? Well, it used to be called Sodom. Not because that's a name to be found in the Bible." She blushed and glanced at the ceiling. She whispered, "Do you suppose he's listening? I wouldn't have him hear this for the world. At that age, anything can corrupt them." She raised her voice. "I can tell you about penalties. Anything you want to know. Just ask me."

He studied her, shrugged, apologetic for his lack of curiosity.

"The penalty for—" she faltered, regained her strength—"certain things we were discussing—back then it was hanging. Now it's life or the chair. Take your pick. Not that you'll have much of a say in the matter."

"Me?"

"A person."

"You could sure get a person over a barrel, Miss Helen, educated woman like you. Whew. Wouldn't want to come up agin you, ma'am."

She twisted her face playfully. "You're poking fun, and I don't blame you. Lord, you'd think I was delivering a valedictory address!"

Jim was not able to help wondering if they had graduated or if there was more to come. He looked at her and saw that he fascinated her. It was as though the bird had hypnotized the snake. He did not like his part, assigned by her, the schoolmarm.

Coldly he said, "So you had to wait and you finally got a ride out and here you are. Better late than never. What's the penalty?"

She was thrown off balance and scared.

"What?"

"For Johnson or the Weidermanns or anybody. Me."

"You?" The trial in town was forgotten, he saw, and saw that she would like to pass judgment on him. He thought he had never seen such naked wanting in anybody's face. But again she managed to sidetrack.

"I got so involved in reading that I missed all of them. Except Pone, who I waited for on Peach Street." She looked as though she could cry. "If anybody from the restaurant saw me, I'm out, that's all."

"I'd be real sorry about that, Helen."

"Why, you wouldn't be to blame. Jim. My goodness." In the drawn-out sentence he thought he could hear her mind clicking. Slowly she said, "It would mean I couldn't keep Jabez. Couldn't keep myself, for that matter, but he would be the first to go, I suppose, for his own good." She promised him, "I'll keep him as long as I can, though."

He wondered if he could trust what he thought he heard. He saw that he could when she suddenly put her finger to her lips and tiptoed over and closed the door. Coming back she told him, "Don't trust him, Jim. His own father told me that. I don't know what it is, but Jay wants something from you. I want your word that when it comes up, you won't let him have it. I admit that I thought—" she stopped, genuinely embarrassed, he could see, then plowed manfully on. "When I came in and found him I admit that I thought things I'd be ashamed to say, to you or anybody. But here you are, innocent as a newborn—"

He shot a mouthful of spit past her to the fireplace, so close to her that she had to dodge it.

"What d'you want? This could go on all day and all night. Fact is, what time I had has just about run out."

She took the challenge. "I wouldn't be in such a hurry if I were you."

"I asked what you want."

"In return for what?"

He thought: my life, my farm? Effie? He said, "What you think you know, maybe? Jabez, free and clear? I haven't hog-tied him anyways that I know about." Taking her tactic, he implied, not knowing where the words could lead. "In the boy's room I found some of your underclothes. What do you reckon a court could say about that?"

She was not surprised, only angry. She spat at him, "He wears them!"

He took a moment following that, but came up, not too feebly, with, "You be willing to tell that to a court?"

She thought about it, said decisively, "No, I wouldn't. People don't understand—" and stopped.

He told her, "That's withholding evidence. Called, if I remember circumstantial. Men have hanged for where it's led." With his eyes he directed her gaze to the sheets. The dilemma was emphasized by a crash from upstairs, probably, Jim thought, a mirror, seven years' worse luck.

He told Helen, "You've been laying for me ever since Ludie left here." He refused to close his eyes on the name. "I'm blamed for her condition. It's aimed I'll pay for it. You've played this one too close to your chest for even a dumb hick like me not to notice and figger it out." He admitted, "It took a long time. Here's something else I know. Effie hasn't been let in on it. All this mystery about who's kin to who." Her face wondered what he meant exactly. "What kind of payment can a man make for such a thing?"

"For Ludie?" She shook her head.

"You ought to know, a thinking woman like you. You shoot or pitch for something, you win it or you don't. If you win it, and you may have, it's what you want or it's not." He brooded over her like a big dark cloud. "I'm asking what it is you want."

She sat in a chair visibly trembling. "Justice. I want some kind of justice."

"For yourself? For Ludie? Or her brother, Jabez?"

He had not been sure until she lowered her head. He saw that he had been mistaken about her ace in the hole.

"Did Jay tell you?"

"No."

"Did you tell him you know?"

"Nobody tells anybody anything. Except you. You were telling me about justice."

"It's just—what's unfair, I want that changed."

"Saying it's not enough. You've got to spell it out, a word at a time. I'm slow." Sorrowfully, not all of it mock, he told her, "Helen, I don't think you trust me to pay up when the time comes."

"You admit there's something to pay up for."

"You wanted justice, you said. For Ludie, wasn't it? I can't pay for something you think. You pay for what you know, I reckon."

"I could know what you know."

"How?"

"I could have him examined by a doctor." She looked up to catch his shock, but he felt as deep inside himself as something in a cave. "All I want," she said, "is your word—" He denied it. She gritted at him, "I want your word that you never—"

"You'll never get it."

She got up and took the clothes from him. "I want your damned word! I want something out of this!"

Unsaid words united them: Is that why he was left here?

They turned away from each other in dislike. At the door she stopped. "Am I some—kind of a—" If she said anything more it preceded her toward the stairs and he did not hear it.

When she had gone he asked the room, "Am I?" He looked around him at the evidence. He thought that the whimpering of the wind sounded just like a fretful baby, tangled in its crib clothes and hungry. He turned his attention to the murmuring above him, heard Helen come down to the kitchen and go back up, heard her sweeping over his head and the sound of broken glass cascading into a metal wastebasket. In a while he heard two sets of footsteps descending, heard one set pause and shift in the kitchen while the other went on out, and then heard it follow. The heavier steps were the ones that almost came to look in on him. The lighter steps had gone on out like a man with money in his pocket.

As though the departed visitors had bored a tunnel through the wind to the barn through which his duty could call, he heard his cattle lowing to be milked.

V

The major storm predicted on the radio did not break in the river valley. The weather gradually cleared and warmed up, though intermittent rain, and the condition of the fields, gave Jim and the other scattered valley farmers a partial vacation of nearly a week. A softer, greener summer returned, the new growth on shrubs and trees and pastures giving it the look of spring.

Several days after their encounter, Jim could not say exactly how many, Helen Taylor came up to the farmhouse to tell Jim that Jabez had got, as she put it, "pretty sick," and she wanted him to know, in case he looked for her in the mornings and did not see her, that she had taken time off from work to tend her nephew. What came out, in a roundabout way as usual, was that Jabez was improving, was sitting up, or had been when she left him, and he wanted her to make sure his boss did not think he was shirking his duties!

Helen was frolicsome and agreeable, even flirtatious. Having taken the measure of his own cunning, Jim told himself as she talked that she had had second thoughts about where temper and the outward signs of suspicion might lead her: out of his house and off of his land. He did not like having her at his mercy, any more than he wanted to be at hers.

When she did not complain, though he waited for it, about the cost to her of having to take the time off, he felt a grudging admiration for her, thinking that she had the right stuff in her to draw on when the going was tough. He saw that she was going to leave him without a hint of the hardship. He thought about her meager salary and her generosity with it, and her efforts to make herself a family out of the leavings of her kin. Having found out the relationship between Ludie and

Jabez, he had reached the conclusion that Jabez was un-
wanted at home as Ludie had been.

The simple and mildly charitable thoughts were a relief to
him after several nights and days of his own dark corners. He
observed Helen's progress down the road flickering with sun-
light and found something in her dumpy back to touch him.

He distrusted himself the minute he acted on his impulse
to call her back. She turned and waited instead. He approved.
Walking up to her, standing toeing a rock as though bashful,
he said, "Effie's been on my tail to do something about that
place of yours. Dunno, looks like women got a club, or some-
thin. Man hasn't got a chance agin 'em."

Helen rushed in. "How is Effie? Has she written to you?"

"Not my wife. The U.S. mails are for herself and her
mama." He thought to make her pay for her diversion, which
had been supposed to recommend her character: his wife's
well-being placed before self-interest. He fell into contem-
plation of the rock and was on the verge of walking off
with an absent-minded "good-by" when she said, "Jim, you
don't have to—I can manage without—"

He snapped his fingers. "Thank you, ma'am. We were talking about your house—" and his second subtle emphasis of
"your" brought a secretive look to her face. He told her,
the generous but gruff farmer, "Place is yours, no rent, until
—well, hell, for the duration, if you want it."

She did not resist coyness. "The duration of the War, sir?"

"I'm damn well not giving you the deed to the place."

She was offended. "I should have told you 'thank you,' but
I didn't. Now I guess I'll say 'No, thank you' and go on the
way I've been doing." Her hand went up to hide her pride as
she swallowed it. "I asked about duration, because nowadays
when anybody says that word they mean until the War is
over." He could see that she wanted to shake her finger, like a
schoolmarm, in his face. "I did not think for a minute that
you were making me a gift of the house, Jim."

He told himself that he had called after her and stopped her
when she was leaving with honor. To lessen the risk of hit-
ting her he mentally stepped to her side.

"Effie said Huffines would give you a job clerking."

She counted her blessings. "I could walk to work in good weather, ride horseback in bad, have time to tend my house and yard, have myself a decent garden."

"O.K." He tipped his hat and walked off.

"I'm very grateful to you." He was sure that four or three days before he would not have heard the undervoice. He gave her a backhand wave.

Rounding his barn he thought about what he had meant by duration. He recalled turning this familiar corner as a stranger that day when he feared he would find a chicken on its back, the chicken that was going to be the death of him. He recalled his fantasy about Effie and the soldier, the pair of guilty lovers. He said, "For the duration, until justice prevaileth."

He imagined that what he had just made was payment, a very small one, no more than so much down. What about that horse she was going to ride to work in bad weather? He laughed out loud. She had no horse, nor a stable to keep it in. You began with the stable, and then you filled the stalls. One horse wouldn't do at all. And look there at the condition of those saddles. English leather is what's wanted here!

Was she strong enough, or was he guilty enough, for further blackmail? After days and nights of ceaseless thought he believed that the payment he had spoken to her about would be his own blackmail of himself. And even as he anticipated and partially planned it, or failed to resist it, he knew that the reason was because he did not intend to settle for the one blackmailable incident but was plotting for more and more opportunities to do the thing he was being blackmailed for: knowing a child in the way the Bible meant when it spoke of knowing a woman. Child was enough to hang him without the addition of *boy*.

It had been as though his brain were oiled. He had grown wily and believed he was gaining knowledge that, if he survived the initial impact, would let him survive anything. His main objective was to beat down the opposing side within him. He had learned some of the methods on the debating team but others, still forming, were undreamed of in Miss Ethel's philosophy. Thinking had become a vice for him. How do you like them apples, Miss Ethel? Once thoughts had been like stones to depress him, but now they were light and porous, deceitfully simple, because examination showed that each thought contained others. He had decided that "to think" was like a hatbox full of letters. The hatbox was the initial thought, and it was in the subsequently opened letters—a lot of them, not all from the same person nor about any of the same things—that pleasure and torment resided.

He wondered about the extent to which he had just been maneuvered by Helen, or outmaneuvered. What percentage of it projected from his mind outward like a rockshelf for her to lean on? Leaning there for support, did she know that the outcropping was not natural but had been crowbarred there by his will, which was looking for punishment? Or had her visit been to make him, through her uncomplained-about hardship, do what he had done? That hand put to her neck to half hide the painful swallow, could have been to draw attention instead of otherwise.

He knew Effie's obvious, harmless tactics backward and forward, but Helen, and all other women, were unknown quantities. All other people. Look at sister Clara, a Northerner who never wrote. Look at Will, a mystery like eternity. And his mother, and Effie's mother, and Ludie. How much of a planned retreat was her craziness, meant to bring him around before it became the real thing?

He would like to know if old straightforward Effie really was the light she had seemed to be through his trials of the past nights when he had wanted to call out for her help. He wished he could believe in it just once more. There are no atheists in foxholes.

Goddamn it, all you did was fuck. Four times, five times. The rain was fucking the earth. Flies rode each other. Worms under the ground.

They don't think. What I am now comes from self-knowledge.

The injunction should have been: Don't know thyself; to thine ownself don't be true—though that was supposed to mean you could not be false to any man. In school he had taken it at face value, assuming with Polonius—a name springing out of the past—that the real core of a man was something good. He could see Miss Ethel's noble expression as she dinned the words into their heads.

What had she been concealing from herself to make the pious expression necessary?

Did she harp on it so much because she hoped the words by themselves could change her and all of them?

Was his unconcern for Jabez, after hearing that the boy was sick, being true or false to himself?

If he covered it up because he was afraid to look at it and conclude that he was responsible, where did that leave him and where did it leave Jabez?

Throughout the ordeal his thoughts of the sex in the afternoon had continued to be brutal. He thought about grip and depth and heat. He had been like a man finding the legendary snapping pussy, which he had always seen in his mind as itself and not connected to a woman with any particular looks or characteristics. He knew that was conditioned thinking. A man always said, "I found me a snapper last night," and it could have been a turtle it was attached to, or a boy. Nobody ever asked what "she" was like; they only inquired about "it."

Just so, he had been concerned only with plumbing the depths and had not thought about, had not given a shit about, the person attached to the source of his release. But the person was the source. If a hole in a rock would have sufficed, Jim would have fucked all the rocks with good holes in the country by now and been content. Animals could have taken him. But the one he wanted to have him was Jabez.

Get on with it. You've shied at this one enough. If it's a snake and it bites you, you know how to handle poison.

He was afraid of finding some tenderness for the kid. The worst part had been when he held the boy's head to his belly and rubbed him down like a little animal hurt in a fight. The fight was o.k., but the feelings were a scar you couldn't hide. Kill but don't kiss.

Fuck but don't love? Everybody does it. Grow up, man.

Look at the kid. Name what you know about him, what you think.

He's experienced.
He has a mind.
He seduced me and took his time doing it.
He's good company.
He makes me think.
Knowing him has changed me forever.

He saw all of his life—old thoughts and aspirations—go rushing past him like long pent-up cattle out of a barn. He had not—this was a killer—until that minute had an idea of the vastness that can lie coiled inside a small act. He was not talking about the sex, which was not small, but was part of the vastness. He meant the small act of saying "hello" to somebody and following that up with other small acts: working together, going to the store together, eating together, tending each other through a bad cold, one person hiring another, befriending another, showing interest in another person.

The whole area of human relationship was trapped like a wood in winter. Only a hermit, living on a barren mountain or plain, was safe.

In his new condition, when he was forced to think about it and make a commitment, he could not see the perversion as amounting to a hill of beans in the bigger scheme, except in the legal sense, and he had never had much respect for lawmakers. He had known most of them hereabouts all of his life, and his inbred contempt, the countryman's contempt, for Washington did not help. At one time or another most of the good old boys he grew up with had tried being cops, and that was always good for a laugh. As they said, if they were all cops at the same time, they couldn't arrest each other, and that would keep the jails nearly empty.

That takes care of the law. You never gave a shit about religion. What's the problem?

He had only scratched the surface today, and there was tomorrow. "Tomorrow and tomorrow—" Miss Ethel, thanks again. It had filled him with dread back then, and a determination to avoid that bleakness in his own life. To avoid it now, as he would fight a snake, he went at the danger head-on with a hoe. Name it, act on it. He sent a silent message to Jabez, defiantly swelling in his clothes. *Get it on up here, boy. Make haste.*

It, still, as though the center of his pleasure were still amputated. For all he could think, that could be what would be done to him when he was found out. Or he might injure Jabez. Freedom, coming late, had made him dangerous. A man like Jim, finding his nature early: Maybe such a man had been right to look for restraints instead of freedom?

He saw that he was supposed now to switch to pondering why Will had gone to Germany, a relief for him, that's how bad things were. The old mystery was meant to lead him away from where he had been: thinking of injuring Jabez permanently as he had injured Ludie, running through that sad family like grease through a goose.

He let his mind quieten down. He wanted an uncluttered place, not too much light, not much noise, everybody tiptoeing. Then let it come. Suppose Effie gets pregnant now and gives me a son?

Jim set out for work with a great tramping, creating for himself with the noise he made the illusion of numbers. A man in a crowd is not so easy to single out and be made into a victim. He saw the crowd at the carnival the night he won the prize meant for him. He was still shooting for a mystery package, and if it was step-ins, or Jesus Christ's autograph, or another cold brass cock, he would not know until he had opened it up.

Out of sight of Jim, Helen Taylor let the day and its central event take her. This weather could make the May apples bloom. She felt like prancing down the road, first this side, then that, highstepping to the oom-pah-pah of the festival air! *My house.*

"Don't crow," she said aloud, sharply, and observed the day more closely than she had on the way up, when nothing except the sense of vague plans had seemed to set it apart.

It was a day when the eye said spring and the nose said autumn. Woody Barnes had set fires going along his damp hedgerows to burn out brambles, and in his washed-out yard patches of rake-exposed topsoil, black and humic and autumnal, sharpened the air. Like a Negro, he had piled tobacco stalks on his lawn to encourage new growth, and there was a smoldering, a brown haze for the nose as though the countryside pulled wetly at a plump cigar of fresh-fired tobacco.

She was astounded by her observations, the easy comparisons flying around like birds let out of a cage. Jabez would be surprised out of his skin! She thought how changed he had been these past days, not just because of the sickness but as though he had grown old beyond his years. Pausing at the edge of the woods, she said, "Now that's not right, taking youth like that," and peered about her for eavesdroppers, to whom she might have added, "A person ought to have to pay for that, damn it."

She stretched as though she were in fact being watched, and let a lyrical gaze affect her face. What the eye saw was April, a sky now high with puffs of wind nudging at clouds as untidy as slept-on pillows, and now, without transition, with its blue swollen by a film of moisture like a child's watercolor on thin paper. When she left Jabez he had been working, writing or drawing, she did not know which, in his secret notebooks. She would give a pretty to have a look inside those notebooks, a stack of them as thick as a big Bible. It would not really be snooping if she had a look, someday when he was out of the house.

Viewed from a distance, courses of waterways could be distinguished by a vaporish green hanging above like clouds of tiny insects. In pastures she had walked on hummocky tan grass, but looking back with the sun saw green there, too, a smear of color in the heart of occasional clumps, as though someone with a long brush dipped in green paint had walked over the fields, dabbing at random, or, leaning on the brush, had paused to rest, tip to heart. It was as though the whole world were being given another chance, to renew itself, to start over, herself included. Barren a week ago, and now look! It made a person dare to make a new stab at what "duration" could mean. *My house.*

Entering the woods, she sat on a log, poised, as it were, on the brink of herself, and stared into her depths, in wonderment at the illusion of riches there. Scenes passed flickering, barely seen previews of coming attractions which she could no more stop than she could fly. A faint voice added: the features to be released only as necessity dictates. Helen and Effie, Wherein Effie Learns about Jim and Ludie. Helen and Jabez, In Which the Reason for Ludie's Craziness Is Explained. Helen and Jim, Wherein—

Again her would-be lyrical gaze sought the air above her, but the still dripping trees offered only somberness, and she was bursting with light, with the need for light and certainty. Jabez's parents had not wanted him, so what came to her because of him was hers alone. She was sorry that she would have to work by herself, but she did not imagine that Effie would be willing to join her, even if given the chance. There was something between men and women who had known each other . . . She, Helen, would have to bring home the bacon solo, but would share it with Effie if anything happened to Jim. That was the very least she could—

Sitting on the log, she whimpered, receiving the import like delayed electrical shocks built into the innocuously familiar seat. Springing up, she fled, as though from the mourners' bench back into the arms of the church. But, slowing down, she encountered predestination, on which she had cut her teeth. What Will Be, Will Be, came to her; and God Moves in Mysterious Ways His Wonders to Perform. Deliberately she walked into a puddle but upon serious reflection decided against total immersion. She had been baptized in a river which had cleansed her sins, not only past but future. Her wet feet—how fittingly, now she looked at it!—would serve to dedicate her future steps to Him, some of Whose Acts were what could be called shady, some of them even resembling blackmail.

She flushed a bird, the Holy Ghost for all she knew, and with full cognizance of the supernatural, watched it fly straight as an arrow for her house. Having just cleared the woods, she stood and watched it circle and tried to will it to settle on the sill of Jabez's window, which would be a sign beyond any mortal quibble. At last, as though feeling the weight of her desire coming into its own, it flew into a tree by *her house*. Like a brown fountain, from the tree a flock of starlings sprang up, and one of them rested on the chosen window sill.

Lena Barnes had brought Jabez a pup to play with, one of a new litter of what she called dash hounds. She hinted that it could be his for keeps. He had no trouble guessing in exchange for what. She arrived so promptly on the moment after Helen's departure that he knew she had been watching and waiting for the opportunity. She reminded him of his mother, plump and clean enough on the surface but with an odor like an unmade bed, complete with used slop jar underneath. They had only chatted across the fence before, once when he was on hinny-watch and again after Effie's visit to him. He knew about the bad blood between her and Effie, and knew that his aunt, out of sympathy for Effie but with no convictions of her own—or so Lena more or less said—also treated Lena like poor white. But this time Lena was after facts, and she pumped him without any attempt to hide her motive. She all but asked him outright if Jim was doing it to Helen. She already knew about Helen staying at Jim's and told Jabez—did he know?—that they met each day and walked up the road, heads together. Her technique was to imply, then decry: "Lord, far be it from me to even suggest—"

He played young, and when she persisted, he played young and sick, and was in fact by the time she had gone feeling nauseated. Her stink, and the way she talked into him as though he were only an amplifier for her own voice and opinions, brought back too many scenes with his mother, Old Typhoid Mary. He had to work hard not to sass Lena, and did not want to get her back up in case she could be useful, but he promised himself more leeway in the future, because he refused to be victimized. If he had learned one thing in the past few days, he had learned that. It was a thing Ludie had tried to teach him when she said, "Hit first, and if you can't, hit hardest." But a victim could hit first or hardest and still be brutalized. Killed. His eyes narrowed in concentration. He owed Jim one, at least, probably a lot more, for killing him. He had had failures and would not tolerate more, for he had been reborn, in pain, and was now, no longer in play-acting terms, and could prove it, "A tough sumbitch, schweethot."

In his final scene with his mother she said, "Why, you've got the meanest eyes I've ever seen looking out of a human head." He said, "How about out of a foot?" and she slapped him, and he walloped her, raising a lump on her face. And still he had been the victim for she had gone screaming to his sexy, tough, heartbreaking old man—Jabez's one real failure, he told himself grimly—and when his father took the strop to him Jabez went for his balls and had his arm nearly broken. He had started for Jim's balls, too, each one the size of a Christmas orange, when Jim was killing him, but had decided that he had rather die under Jim, whatever the method of death, than live on as his enemy at a distance, seeing, wanting, and denied. And he had perished.

The newborn boy felt differently, though the differences were as yet vague and varied. *Newborn*, not resurrected like Lazarus. The old kid was dead and buried in that bedroom, able only to haunt and terrify.

Jim knew he had killed him. He had asked, "Why did you go away to die?"

Fondling the pup, putting it to his breast in parody and yet not, he looked at the small worried face and wondered what kind of deal it was going to get. Was it in the pup's future to go mad and foam and slather and infect the countryside until it was caught and killed? Or could the love of a good man save it?

He was saving himself, his strength and best efforts, for the ordeal ahead, which would be when Helen had gone off to the wedding and he and Jim were alone. He did not know quite what he wanted, but sometimes in his reveries he could see himself and someone else who might be Jim, traveling. Jabez longed to see the ocean. Today, after the long separation, he hoped the other person would be Jim. They had not even exchanged their first kiss.

Helen had told him that Jim said, "I haven't hog-tied Jabez anyways that I know about." She asked him to explain what that meant. He did not explain, but played the kid until he could have puked on her by his bedside. She actually, straightening his sheets, suddenly jabbed her finger at his asshole, and when he yelled, looked like she knew something worth knowing.

"I'm sore from the diarrhea," he said coldly, hating her guts. The fact that he explained made her look smugger than before. He wanted to tell her, "I don't care what you think or what you know. I'd let him fuck me in front of you, and in front of Miss F. and the whole goddamned county. If he wanted to, I'd be in a carnival sideshow with him." Because he was, however temporarily, tied up, and Jim knew it or it would not have come to him to say he wasn't. The hog-tier was just as involved as the one he tied up, and Jim knew that, too.

Of course, it might not be temporary, that was a possibility. When he had Jim away from here and they were beside seas upon which Greek lovers in pairs had gazed, it might occur to a languid and satiated Jabez that here, precisely, was what he wanted, and he would tell Jim, and watch Jim's hopeless look turn fierce and blinding with the knowledge of possession, by and of. A hut or a palace, it would not matter; and Jabez could see himself astride Jim's broad back, a little jockey breaking in his mount. Jim's frightened loathing of being subjected had, after the fact, to the sensibilities of the new Jabez, presented a challenge that was increasingly arousing. And though he knew the difference between fantasy and action, that they were frequently opposites—humanitarians daydreaming murder—when he thought of cornholing Jim a real brutal manhood stirred in him. He would not fight it if, like a root in a cellar, it wanted to grow in darkness. The old boy had been a hunter, but the new boy could imagine himself hunting a different sort of quarry. Jim had a lot to learn, all right.

Jabez was realistic. He told the pup, "I'm too young to know what I'll want next year. I could be in Timbuctoo, or in Hoptown in the asylum with Ludie." He grinned at his old way of thinking. It would be hard to break, but he was free of that worry, at least, newborn of himself without parents to infect him. "Or I could be under a freight train on my way to someplace. You and me, it's no good for us to try to plan too far ahead. Two-three weeks is as far as we ought to look. By that time you'll be weaned. By then, I may be sucking. You can sleep between us." The pup wriggled under the covers, sniffing out a place of approximate familiarity. Jabez told it, "You may not want what you're shooting for down there, old buddy. But you won't know 'til you've won it."

A starling lit on his window sill and officiously marched along it, trying out the cracks in the screen with its beak, attempting to uproot an old staple which it may have thought was a rigid acrobatic worm.

The pup settled between Jabez's legs, sighed and mewled and went to sleep. Softly Jabez said to it, "You and me, we're still kind of at their mercy."

He saw himself grown old, grayhaired, mustached, epaulets on his shoulders, a figure of boundless authority, IN CONTROL of his life.

He drew his new notebook to him, unscrewed the top of the big fountain pen he had stolen from his father's clothes, and after a time of deep reflection, he opened the book and wrote, dating it two weeks ahead.

"Today I move in with Jim. Aunt Helen is leaving this morning on the milk truck to attend the wedding of Miss Effie's sister, Junie. She will be gone for two nights. I was surprised when Jim said to me, yesterday, that we would have to sleep in the same bed. It may be that he thinks about me as somebody to replace his dead brother, though I don't know if they slept together, or what."

Turning the page he made another entry for the same day, writing in LATE AFTERNOON. "Jim took the afternoon off from work and we sat in the house and talked. We had something to drink, I think it was liquor, and I got sleepy. He kept saying how sleepy he was and asking me if I didn't want to get in the bed. It was ignamatical."

He crossed out and wrote correctly above the misspelled

word, an authentic touch for those seeking proof of some kind. "He *always—*" his aunt's voice; was it in a courtroom? —"always said the word that way."

Idly he turned to the middle of the book and started to write, but tore out the leaf, saying, "There'll be plenty of real stuff." After meditation it seemed that something more was called for, something rather theatrical, because he was feeling bored. He flipped the pages trying to catch a glimpse of fleeting images not yet impressed there, as though it were one of those little books of cartoons that gave an illusion of motion when the pages were rapidly riffled with the thumb. Coming to the last sheet, after a long spell of weighing and rejecting during which with regret he heard his aunt enter the house and approach the stairs, he wrote, in big but shaky letters like someone at the end of his time:

I CAN NO LONGER AFFORD MY LIFE

Giggling, he lay back and feigned sleep. Hearing his aunt's cautious tread on the stairs, he imagined for a moment that the final words had been written by Jim, driven by Jabez to a desperate, perhaps fatal, act.

As though waking to his aunt's fond gaze and being startled by it, he shoved the notebook under the covers with the pup and saw Helen's eyes flicker with greed. He must wear the notebooks like clothes until he was ready for her to find them. With distaste, he saw that for all the avarice, her gaze was genuinely fond enough to make him bilious. She seemed actually to be doting on him. He let his eyes flutter blue innocence.

"What was my treasure dreaming about? Is he better now?"

In reverse sequence he answered her. "I'm almost well. I was dreaming about Miss Effie's garden." He smiled gently, fatigued but convalescent. "My job."

One evening in late summer Jim Cummins came to the schoolteacher. To the fourth tap on the door she called out faintly, "It's open," and then he was in the room with her. He was afraid his large shadow looming in the dusk would scare her, but an easily scared woman would not have left her door open in a town that, since the War ended, had had its share of burglaries and mischief, mostly against lone women. He looked on her frailness with pity and hoped it would not show in his voice. He identified himself to her and took a seat by the couch on which she lay making hardly more of a heap than a child would.

"I hadn't heard from you in a while," he said, "s'why I came." But her old spirit was still in her and she challenged him.

"You've heard about me, though."

"Well—" he said, but her directness made him continue. "They say you go around town talking to me, calling others by my name." It said it drolly.

She was snappish. "Some words travel faster than others."

"Gossip. Bread and meat to some."

"You, apparently, among them."

He was easy. "Wanted to hear it firsthand, that's all. Woman going around talking to a man that ain't there, she's going to bring that fella to her, 'less he's dead."

"Sometimes the dead come quicker than the living."

In any other mouth the words could have made his flesh crawl, but because it was her, he listened and heard the truth. Hardly a week passed that he didn't talk, in a manner of speaking, to shades. And sometimes, in response to his words, they became more than shades, were plain enough for him to make out features. His living wife, sitting darning socks, would, because of some answer he made her that he had once made to another, become that other person, and he would have to shake his head like a dog to get shed of the image. So he agreed with her.

"We've got to be careful who we call up."

"What we've got to be careful of is *why* we call them up. Motive, Jim, is the most dangerous thing in the world."

Her need to have the final word, to alter every thought, made him smile, remembering how her pupils had called her The Fascist. But one thought led to another that proved her right. He considered Hitler's motive, and the results that were still stunning the world. People hereabouts were trying to deny what the papers carried, for it reflected to a terrible degree upon their involvement in the War, their losses, and the complicity of their leaders. Their pride and dignity were being drained off like water from a sinkhole to reveal something putrid and bottomless. His old teacher wasn't the only one to go around talking to somebody not there. Into his thoughts her voice came like a bird's at nightfall, a "cheep" asking for an answering "cheep."

"Jim, I've done something dangerous."

"*You*, Miss Ethel?"

"No, *no*. It is *I*, Jim. She's—" He saw a flutter like a moth settling on the couch by her hand. "She's wandering around."

He gentled her. "You want me to put her out, like the cat?"

"She's smaller than a cat. About the size of a butterfly."

He wondered what she meant, wondered if turning on a lamp would bring them both a little closer to everyday. When she amplified her remark she did not throw any light on her meaning.

"She's just a signature, and a forgery at that." She sounded excited as though she had discovered something. "So many signatures set loose in a lifetime! All of them fluttering around, each one carrying identification, saying, as I have, 'It is I, it is *I*.' There's a valley in Greece, a valley of butterflies. A gathering place for all our signatures? I would have liked to have seen all mine. I'm sure—" and she sounded like his wife, clucking over a secret—"that I could find *myself there* more easily than closer to home." She nodded, sounding amused, at another part of the room.

"Let's go," he said, pretending to get up.

"The two of us, together in Greece?" She mocked him and said, like a quote, "And they were beside seas upon which Greek lovers in pairs had gazed—" then sat up crying out, "What?" as if somebody had answered.

For both their sakes' he snapped on a light. She threw her hand up, but he thought it was not so much on account of the sudden glare as to keep him from seeing her, her long face longer because she was so thin, her thin hair not combed, her skin powdery. The ones who told him she was going around calling strangers by his name had said she looked wild, but he had not been able to imagine that extremely neat woman as other than she had been. For once, people had not exaggerated.

What he wanted to do, what he could not do, was pick her up like a kid and take her out to the truck and drive her back to the farm and force-feed her. He questioned the denial in the thought, saw that it came from the idea of picking her up in his arms. He grinned respectfully at his awe, rooted in what she had been, a woman available in many ways but carrying around her a thing like a fence with a sign on it NO ADMISSION BEYOND THIS POINT. The awe had outlasted another feeling, brought to the front now because of her downfall. He recalled how the idea of testing the sincerity of that sign had been put in his mind by schoolmates, girls, naturally, who had implied that they thought he and the teacher were doing it. Girls, naturally. Boys would have thought of their mothers and kept quiet, as they didn't about younger teachers. Girls had said they "bet she would," putting themselves in her place at her age, he reckoned, recognizing that he was not one of the mother-humbled ones. And he had thought about it, about her virginity as a prize, and had been excited and eager. He recalled bringing up the subject of sex, one evening when they had been partly hid from each other by the dusk, and her blankness except for two spots of color on her cheeks that shone in the twilight.

"I have no relations in that part of the country." Was that what she said? His disappointment had made him very uncomfortable and had led, he saw now, to his desertion. He had been so sure of her! He had imagined her coming across in two ways: jumping on him, and calmly, a woman of the world, leading him to her bed. The woman of the world had been an ideal, the hardest to imagine . . . Her arms were round in her summer dresses, and though the skirts were long, what he could see of her legs looked good in the nylons, no veins showing. Smooth virgin legs that had never wrapped around the back of any man. He had thought a lot about running his cheek, stubbly and maybe exciting to her, all the way from her ankle up to the notch.

He saw that she was watching him and wondered how much of what he was thinking had showed on his face. He gave her another look that said how her clay touched him still, that he was a man who would plant there because it was in his nature to hate the idea of anything lying fallow. But her friability was the powder left by drought, and even an earthworm moving in that soil would be as destructive to it as an atomic bomb.

"I've maligned you," she said.

Under the words he thought he heard a plea for the consequences of slandering somebody.

"That's not what I've been told."

"I don't mean in words. Well, not spoken."

He gave her his attention.

"In secret. A long secret winter of thoughts followed by a hell of a spring and summer of scribbling."

"I think, too," he told her, finding it far out of the ordinary that she was speaking his thoughts to that extent. The two of them, with secret thoughts about each other. But he saw that she was only expressing the most natural thing he could think of, had made it seem mysterious because she was who she was. Of course people spoke far less about each other than they thought. If all thoughts were spoken . . . but that was the most unimaginable thing.

"Do you *write*, Jim? Do you keep logs, journals, diaries in which you write down wishes instead of events, for all the wrong reasons, for someone to read in the future and take for facts?"

He shook his head. "I don't have time for that."

"I do. I have. I've written a life that could put you behind bars, if lived."

"Anything can happen. I remember those two roads in the wood."

"It was the poet's decision. I gave you no choice. Arbitrarily, I pushed you down another road."

"Not me," he said, knowing his life, then, "Why?"

Her sigh was as heavy as an old animal's dying behind a stove.

"If I knew that, I could let go. I'm hanging on here like something caught in a web but not eaten, growing so dry you can see through me, asking for something to finish me off." In her bright-eyed look he saw that she had said something that satisfied her. "Yes, that's literal. I'm looking for somebody to finish me off, to finish my story for me! Have I found him? Has he found me? It was you sought me out, Jim!"

She tried to get up, tried to hide from him the fact that she could not. He wondered how long she had been lying there because she had to, and sniffed as though his nose might tell him, but there was no odor that his farm-accustomed nose might have earlier overlooked. But the idea was enough for him, and he launched at her a lie that he would make good if he had to kill his wife, who didn't like the teacher at all.

"My wife sent me in here to fetch you back with me. She said not to come home if I was aiming to come by myself."

"How kind!" He heard her intention, which was to shut him up. He refused her.

"Now, I respect my wife and I like my own bed. You may be dangerous as all get out, like you say you are, but I think you'll agree I could put up a pretty good fight—"

Her interruption was weak as if her strength were being sapped by something underground. "Where will you put me, in your mother's death room, or the room from which Will went to his death? The room where Jabez stood watching you with too much knowledge, which can be death? It was the second day of the storm. He looked at you through his fever, through tree limbs like bones."

"I don't think I know that feller." He got up slowly, not to frighten her, and stretched the arms that would soon be carrying her to his truck. He wanted to lift her up and hold her for a minute, pressed to him with her disgraceful head against his neck, in the room where she had teased his mind and his body with thoughts that involved a world he had never seen except through her. What he had half learned in that room had puzzled him and amused her, for she had handed him logic and metaphysics on the same platter and had smiled to see the country boy try to eat both with his knife. He believed that the half learning had kept him alive and made him sometimes wish he could be dead. He saw the impulses as the same thing. Yes, he would like to punish her for too much and too little given. She was always so opinionated. He recalled from a book she had lent him: Opinions make people cruel.

"I'm remembering too much," he told her, preparing her. But she was still the teacher, still The Fascist.

"There may be worse things than memory." With her old bossiness she pointed to a bureau, told him what drawer, under what pile of clothes. He brought the thick sheaf of paper, held together with rubber bands, to her and sat when ordered to. Smoothing the paper, she looked like somebody dowsing for water.

"In here are some lives. Some lies, too, but that's no contradiction."

The thickness of the stack of paper gave his words bitterness. "If there is one, *God* knows that's the truth."

He knew there was no mistake. She meant for him to read this wad of words as she watched. He estimated that dawn would look in on him reading.

She told him, "An old woman's revenge. I place my life in your hands." She settled her head back on the pillows. He measured her frailty, letting her see. A flicker in her eyes told him she would be grateful. He had a thought that he marked like a place in a book: "You can't have everything." The remark was addressed to her, a woman who had not had much of anything. There she lay, unplowed, unseeded, unreaped, her breath shallow as a sick baby's.

He read: "The dinner bell rang across the dusty tobacco field, catching Jim between the shoulder blades like a rusty knife," and riding above the line were two words, the most frightening that he knew: crib death.

Soon enough he saw that her "I have no relations in that part of the country" was one of the lies, for it looked like she had no relations anywhere else. He kept glancing at her, making connection between her and what he was reading. Her nature was spread out before him like a field, like a whore. That bundle of bones, beginning to snore like a man, was word by word contradicting everything he had been taught about a woman's nature, or thought he wanted to believe. He saw how she was scattered through the book, in disguises meant to fool herself: as Ludie, as Jabez—telling him about her feeling for him. He read the book as a confession: that she could have been the woman for him, or the boy, if that was the way he tended. He wondered, glancing at her from time to time, if she knew what she was doing, if that was why she gave him the book to read. It was plain for him to see, plain enough, that the book was *their* story, or was that because he wanted to see it, the wanting growing out of a boastful streak? In places she pegged him to the board, in others she was so off the mark it didn't matter to him what she wrote. Those were the parts he imagined she thought were "dangerous." In Will, who died for sex, he saw her signature plainest: Will, the fascist. Whose will wasn't a one-party dictatorship? He thought she maligned not him but herself, not through confession but through the coldness that made her deny what she was, in all but words. But what a woman she could have been!

As though she dictated even his current responses, at the thought of taking her before it was too late he stirred in his manhood, mentally and physically. Would she, in her fatigue, survive him, or would he end her life by fucking her to death? Then she would be that victim she harped so much on in the course of the book. She had asked him to finish her life. For such a woman, maybe the loss of virginity would be the same as death.

Then, as he read, he watched her lose that virginity, give it up, spread it around in bits of gristle and blood, for the toughest hymen was in the mind. As if she knew what she had done, she told him—in her own book, in her own words, in her own hand—I CAN NO LONGER AFFORD MY LIFE.

He asked her, "Do you know what's *in* here?" He saw that dawn lay on the carpet powdery and unkempt as she was. He saw her eyes fixed on him, waiting for a verdict. He told her, "I see a lot. I wanted you, too." Then, for there was no flicker, he asked anxiously, "Do you hear me?" and saw that unlike the dawn she would not wax into another day. Once he had left her, cheating her. She had got back at him. He wondered if he had "finished" her life by looking at it, as she had asked him to do. He suspected it was so, because some lives are too fragile to withstand another's recognition. He was the only man to recognize her. She had asked him to. Finally, woman of the world, she had led him to her bed. He could not think any more about it.

He held her then.

repetition of bed scene
in AA — overlap w/ dressing bathroom undressing
pattern.